SPELLS OF UNDEATH

A CAVAN OLTBLOOD NOVEL

STEFON MEARS

Also by Stefon Mears

Cavan Oltblood Series
Half a Wizard
The Ice Dagger
Spells of Undeath

Spells for Hire
Devil's Shoestring
Zombie Powder
Spirit Trap
Dragon's Blood (coming December 2019)

The Rise of Magic
Magician's Choice
Sleight of Mind
Lunar Alchemy
Three Fae Monte
The Sphinx Principle

The Telepath Trilogy
Surviving Telepathy
Immoral Telepathy
Targeting Telepathy

Edge of Humanity
Caught Between Monsters
Hunting Monsters

Power City Tales
Not Quite Bulletproof
No Money in Heroism

Devil's Night
Portal-Land, Oregon
Stealing from Pirates
Fade to Gold
With a Broken Sword
Twice Against the Dragon
The House on Cedar Street
Sudden Death
On the Edge of Faerie
Confronting Legends (Spells & Swords Vol. 1)
Uncle Stone Teeth and Other Macabre Poems
The Patreon Collection, Vol. 1-4 (Vol. 5, coming soon)

Published by Thousand Faces Publishing, Portland, Oregon

http://1kfaces.com

ISBN: 978-1-948490-01-6

SPELLS OF UNDEATH

A Cavan Oltblood novel

1

———————

Once more, Cavan Oltblood found himself running half-naked through the chilly midnight streets of a small town, pursued by armed men with violence in mind.

This time, the town was Drien, and the streets were not mere dirt, but irregular cobblestones drawn from the nearby river.

Unfortunately, that just meant that Cavan's calf-high leather boots made more noise. Another small thing, working against his escape.

Just like the beautiful full moon in the cloudless sky above. Only a few hours ago, during the harvest festival, that moon had been romantic. Mood-setting, even. Brought him apple-and-honey kisses that led to yet more sweetness.

Now, all that moonlight just made Cavan easier to spot.

Well, if he had to run through midnight streets again, at least this time he was wearing pants.

He was even pretty sure he had all his belongings, hurriedly wrapped in his gray cloak, once the shouting had started from downstairs.

At the very least, Cavan knew for a fact he had his sword, his armor, his pouch of spells and his pouch of coins.

If he'd lost his good red tunic, well, the world wouldn't end.

Cavan lowered his head for a burst of speed, and took a tight corner to try to put some distance between himself and those men-at-arms.

Alas, the buildings of this town were inconveniently far apart, when it came to fleeing from pursuit. Didn't these people ever worry about invading armies?

The buildings themselves were no help either. All wooden construction — pine, from the nearby forest — and not nearly enough two and three-story buildings that would cast longer shadows.

Not that shadows would have helped much. Not close as those pursuers were.

Cavan could hear the men-at-arms no more than a street or so behind him. Their shouts, their pounding boots. He could even glimpse the light of their torches, if he dared to look back once more.

No point in that, though. Any more than Cavan saw a point in trying to figure out where all those men-at-arms had come from, who they worked for, or how they had found him so quickly.

For that matter, Cavan wasn't even sure why they were after him.

Reesa, the young lady who had been so eager to share her charms with Cavan, had most definitely not been married, nor promised to anyone. She'd assured him twice.

Also, Cavan had checked around, subtly. Gotten confirmation over the course of the evening from a couple of serving girls who knew Reesa.

This wasn't Myrapek, after all, where what some places called "infidelity," the Myrese called "a bit of harmless fun."

Cavan hadn't even broken any laws in Drien. Not that he knew of, at least.

And Ehren had run down a pretty long list of the local ordinances during their ride into town. Ehren had made especially clear that, in Drien, only the town wizard could cast spells without both a local residence and a separate permit for each spell.

In fact, that warning was the entire reason that Cavan didn't use any of the rain barrels he passed to conjure a mist that would hide his escape. Not to mention give him time to finish getting dressed.

No. No spells. He had trouble enough right now without breaking the law.

So Cavan had to choose between running and fighting at least a half-dozen armed men. Them with rings of mail sewn into leather jerkins that hung all the way to their knees, while Cavan's sleeved hauberk and leggings of magnificent *licha* were wrapped in his cloak, where they would do him no good at all in a fight.

Could he have beaten those men-at-arms anyway? Quite possibly. This was a small town, in the equally small kingdom of Oinos. Not likely to produce the level of opposition Cavan had grown used to in his travels.

But Cavan wasn't likely to defeat those men-at-arms without killing at least some of them. And despite Ehren's accusations that Cavan was getting more and more like Amra, he really did try not to kill anyone he didn't have to.

So Cavan lowered his head again, and put on another burst of speed, cutting around the next corner, to the left, and hoping that the covered cart at that corner would provide cover.

Not just a simple sheet of roughspun stretched across an open, flat cart, but multiple sheets sewn together over a framework that look tall enough that even Cavan might have been able to stand up on that cart.

By all rights, it should have been more than enough to hide his escape.

But Cavan's luck never quite worked that way.

He rounded the corner and was immediately grabbed by strong hands.

His back was slammed against a rough wooden wall before he even saw who grabbed him.

Amra. Of course.

More than a head shorter than Cavan. Clad in the tight black leathers that showed off her curves as well as protected them. Her wyrding greatsword slung over her shoulder. Her quirking smile, amused at Cavan's plight.

Tanned skin, curly black hair, green-and-gold eyes ... and lethal skills and tendencies. That was Amra.

"Unbelievable." That was spoken by Qalas, with his dark black southern skin and his rare, dark blue eyes. He still wore his old studded leather armor, but his tight black curls had grown longer since he quit his service to the Duke of Nolarr. And Qalas had begun growing a beard since they'd started north.

Qalas held his halberd in one hand, and with the other he tossed a pouch into the air for Amra to catch. "How could you possibly have known?"

"I warned you," Ehren's voice, Cavan could hear the smile, as well as the baritone he knew so well. "Never bet against Amra. She only bets when she's sure she's right."

"Which is always," Amra said, hefting the pouch of coins with evident pleasure.

"In military matters, perhaps," Ehren said, and now Cavan saw the smiling priest over to his right, leaning against the wall beside the cart. As always, Ehren's pale skin, long sun-blond hair, and white clothing were spotless, all the way down to his doeskin boots. A mark of favor from his deity, the sun goddess Zatafa.

Ehren gestured with his smooth, goldenwood staff. "However—"

"Where are the horses?" Cavan interrupted as he hustled for the rest of his clothing. And more importantly, his armor.

The *licha* armor, shades of tan and red, forged from deepsand and steel by a dune elf smith into material so smooth it might have been woven. Lighter than the cloth of Cavan's clothing, but stronger than an anvil.

And it did look good over his lean muscles and swarthy skin.

The tunic wasn't there. Oh, well. He might lose some arm and chest hair to the armor then.

"Where else would the horses be? At the inn," Amra said, blinking innocently. "We're not leaving until Caramel is reshod, and that won't be before morning."

"Besides," Ehren added, "you know I don't like starting a ride without the glory of Zatafa on the rise."

Cavan was still trying to decide on his rejoinder when the men-at-arms rounded the corner.

THE FULL MOON ALMOST DIRECTLY OVERHEAD. HARDLY A CLOUD IN THE midnight sky, though a large crowd of stars kept watch. The smell of smoke from harvest festival fires still on the breeze.

Cavan, finishing buckling on his sword belt, with his *licha* armor properly back between himself and harm. His loose-woven gray cloak already draped over his shoulders, and fixed into place with its clasp, done in the county seal of Juno: the blue mountain was carved from actual crystal mined from the Ice Dagger, the mightiest peak of the Blue Mountain range. The rest of the clasp was gold.

He at least felt presentable when the men-at-arms rounded the corner.

Ehren remained where he was, leaning casually against the wall of ... whatever building that was. No door on this side, but with that covered cart at the corner, Cavan was betting on a shop or a tavern.

No. Had to be a shop. Cavan couldn't imagine a tavern dead enough that he wouldn't hear some kind of raucous noise, with the streets this quiet. At least that meant the men-at-arms weren't likely to have supporters come out at the first sound of clashing steel.

Qalas only shifted his grip on his halberd. Kept its steel-wrapped butt on the cobblestones, and its axe and spike threatening no one, but Cavan recognized the grip. Qalas would be able to strike just as quickly from that pose as he would if he'd been holding it aloft.

Amra took nothing like a combat stance at all. She just smiled as she made a show of counting the men-at-arms as they spread out across the wide street.

Cavan was at least pleased to see more than half of them sweating and panting for breath.

"A dozen? That's all? And they only have maces. Not even

flanged maces." Amra turned to Cavan, a sour expression on her face. "I expect better from you, Cavan. Even if they're any good, which I doubt, there are hardly enough of them for a satisfying fight. Unless ... maybe ... if you and Qalas want to stand aside and watch?"

Ehren cleared his throat and took a step forward, adjusting the soft leather backpack he kept with him always.

"Now, gentlemen," Ehren began.

He didn't get to finish.

One of the men-at-arms, the oldest and evidently the leader, blew three sharp blasts on a hunting whistle.

"Hisst," Amra said, hands raised to hush him. "You'll draw the watch and spoil our fun."

The man with the whistle stared at Amra as though he couldn't believe what he was hearing.

"We *are* the town watch," he said. He slapped his upper left shoulder, where something was in fact sewn over the rings and leather.

Now that Cavan looked at the patches, he could see that they did look like the Drien seal. Pale green squares checked by pale blue. A couple of the men-at-arms, or rather, the *watchmen*, lowered their torches to show off their badges.

Sure enough, every one of the dozen had that seal.

"Cavan," Ehren started, in that irritated tone Cavan had brought out of his friend all too many times over the years.

Cavan didn't let him finish.

"I didn't cast a *thing*! I haven't broken *any* laws since I came to town. I swear."

Hoofbeats. Cavan could hear them, even as he tried to demand the watch sergeant tell him what was going on.

At least three or four horses, approaching at speed.

The watch sergeant just gave Cavan a grim look for an answer, and shook his head.

Amra sighed and looked at Ehren. "You're going to get pissy if I kill them, aren't you?"

"What *is* this about?" Ehren said, stepping between the watchmen and Cavan. And between the watchmen and Amra, for that matter. "If Cavan says he's broken no laws, then he hasn't."

"Nice to be so sure," the sergeant of the watch said. He smiled at something farther along the street. "You'll see soon enough."

Cavan glanced back and saw more watchmen at the other end of the street. At least twice as many at that end.

He and his friends were well and truly penned in now.

"Better," Amra said, nodding, after she saw the approaching guards. "Now we may not have to try very hard, but at least we'll all get to play."

"Ehren," Cavan muttered, "if I'm going to be falsely accused, I'm going to start casting."

"Peace," Ehren said, jaw set and strain in his features, and yet his small smile still in place. But before he could say anything more, those horses arrived.

An older, aristocratic man in fine clothes rode the lead horse. His dark blond hair was going white, but he looked to have strength in his limbs to swing the longsword he wore at his side.

More watchmen on horses with him. A half-dozen. And these had lances in their hands, and crossbows strapped to their saddles.

"I'm so sorry about this, Cavan," called a voice Cavan had gotten to know quite well over the last several hours.

A high, clear voice that sounded lovely when singing, and even lovelier when engaged in ... other activities.

Craning a bit, Cavan could see her seated on the horse behind the older man. The pale blue dress she wore now had a far more conservative cut than the gown she'd worn to the harvest festival, though she still made it look fetching. Might have helped that her long, honey blond hair hung wild about her shoulders.

"Reesa," Cavan said, "you swore you weren't married or promised."

She gave an apologetic shrug. At least the look in her eye suggested that she had an explanation, if Cavan ever got to hear it.

That was something, at least, Cavan supposed.

"You are Cavan Oltblood," the aristocratic man said, but not like it was a question. "Bastard son of King Draven of Oltoss, and future Count of Juno."

Reesa's eyes and mouth widened in shock, so at least *she* hadn't known Cavan was anything more than a wanderer in search of adventure.

So how did this old man know so much?

"And you are..." Cavan said, which got him a dirty look from Ehren and a snicker from Amra, her green-and-gold eyes dancing in the torchlight. Qalas just kept his eyes on the watch.

"Draig, fourth son of Baron Essell, and heir to his barony, as well as Speaker for the Council of Drien."

"You couldn't find a willing tavern wench?" Qalas muttered. "Farmer's daughter, perhaps?"

"It seems my daughter has misled you," Draig continued. "She is, in fact, as of this very morning, promised to the first son and heir to the county of Vulyys." Draig spared his daughter a dark look. "A betrothal spoiled by her activities tonight, unless I take swift action."

"I never agreed to that match," Reesa said, matching her father's dark tone admirably. "And it wasn't due to be revealed publicly before morning. So—"

"So you seem to have chosen a match for yourself."

"That's not what I was going to say. Father, if you'd listen—"

Draig silenced her with a gesture and turned a malevolent smile on Cavan. "Well done, my daughter. A future count, and potential future king."

"Hardly," Cavan said, unable to stop himself. "Even if my half-brothers and sisters all died, there's no way the—"

"So you don't object to the marriage part?" Amra said, laughing. "This Reesa must be something else between the—"

"Cavan Oltblood," Draig said, his tone formal. "Will you marry my daughter under the first rays of Zatafa? Or shall I conclude that the Kingdom of Oltoss is interfering in politics here in the Kingdom of Oinos, and have you arrested for espionage?"

FALSE ACCUSATIONS BY MOONLIGHT. YES, THAT SOUNDED LIKE CAVAN'S luck.

A dozen members of the town watch at the near side of the street. All with maces in their hands, if not actively menacing, though at least they looked winded from chasing Cavan through the streets.

Twice that many watchmen at the other end of the street. Moving slowly closer.

Plus, this Draig, Speaker for the Council of Drien, had another six watchmen on horseback beside him. All with lances ready. Not to mention crossbows strapped to their saddles.

The lingering hints of smoke in the air made Cavan wonder if they had a pyre waiting for him. He recognized that thought, though, as the darkness of the moment. That smoke remained from the harvest festival bonfires.

At least Reesa, pretty Reesa, looked to be innocent, and not trying to set him up for this accusation of espionage.

"Quite a stretch," Qalas said, hefting his halberd. "Two people meet at a festival, and you call it espionage?"

"Trumped up charges and a rigged trial?" Amra drew her two-handed sword with its mysterious dark blade, harder than steel. "You'll forgive us if we resist."

The assembled guards all readied their weapons.

Cavan reached for his pouch of spells.

"Wait!" Ehren cried out, raising both hands to hold his golden-wood staff high.

It seemed for a moment as though Ehren stood in a shaft of pure sunlight, despite the hour.

But he had everyone's attention.

"You say you revere Zatafa," Ehren said, directing his words to Draig. "Well I am her priest, and you may judge my standing by my clothing."

Ehren turned in place once, slowly.

A few of the guards whistled admiration at the way Ehren's crisp, white clothes bore not a single mote of dust.

"Very well," Draig said. "You can only be the priest known as

Ehren. Companion of Cavan's, but clearly you have Zatafa's favor. Speak your piece."

"I wish only to ask a question, and hear it answered." He looked past Draig. "Reesa, what is it *you* want?"

"I think we *all* know what she—" Amra started but Cavan elbowed her in the stomach. She didn't lose that grin though.

Reesa jumped down from the horse. A smooth, agile movement that told Cavan she had more than a little experience on horseback.

"Reesa," Draig began, but Ehren waved him to silence. Draig bristled, but his own town watch muttered objections, and respect for the priest.

Draig swallowed his irritation.

"Reesa," Ehren said again, and Cavan knew the penetrating stare of Ehren's clear blue eyes all too well. He could only imagine what Reesa must be experiencing, facing it for the first time.

She held her back straight, though, and her chin defiant.

Was it wrong that Cavan found her even more attractive like that, than he had while she danced with him at the festival?

"I could ask you many questions," Ehren continued. "Why you misled my friend tonight. If you knew the full truth of my friend's identity before you took him to your bedchamber. If you sought to trap my friend in a political dispute."

Ehren shook his head. "None of those questions, though, matter so much as the one question I do ask. And I wish to know the answer. What is it *you* want?"

"I never wanted my mother's life. Running a noble household. Arranging parties and playing politics." She turned to her father. "Let Ansa and Dula live that life. I crave the open road. Adventure. There is so much to see and do out in this world. I don't want to live and die here in this tiny kingdom. Our borders aren't more than a week's journey from the Wailing Woods, but I've never even seen an elf!"

Fury thundered in Draig's eyes as Reesa continued.

She turned her attention to Cavan, urgency in her soft gray eyes. "Those stories you told. They're all true, aren't they?"

"If I know Cavan," Amra said before Cavan could answer, "he didn't exaggerate a word of whatever he told you."

"If anything," Qalas added, "he probably played down his own role in events."

"It's true," Ehren said, giving Cavan a smile. "Cavan has many faults, but braggadocio isn't one of them."

"Then take me with you. I'm good with a bow, and—"

"*Enough!*" Drien bellowed. "That will be quite enough of this foolishness. Priest, I have granted your request. Your question, asked and answered. But my fidelity to Zatafa does not mean I must forsake generations of tradition and the needs of my own family by sending my eldest daughter out to die in the wilderness because of a few stories and a pair of brown eyes."

"Father!" Reesa objected.

"No," He said, his voice as final as the grave. "Well, Cavan Oltblood? Marry her and you may take her on all the adventures you wish. Refuse, and face trial for espionage."

"I never agreed to marry anyone!" Reesa said, but it was rage in her words and eyes, not pleading. "He couldn't have known what you'd arranged."

"Couldn't he?" Draig said. "I'd say a trial could determine what a resourceful man like Cavan Oltblood knew and what he did not when he sought you out at the festival."

"Oh, *enough*," Amra said. "No more politics. It gives me a headache. You seem to know Cavan and Ehren. Do you know who I am?"

"Your reputation as both a warrior and a commander precedes you, Amra," Draig said, his tone more careful now. "And I know your fourth as Qalas, former hunter for Duke Falstaff of Nolarr, in the kingdom of Oltoss."

Qalas looked surprised to be recognized, but said nothing.

Amra, however, continued.

"Good. Then hear this. *I'm* not of a mind to let *anyone* be forced into marriage. Certainly not my friend Cavan, and not this spirited girl in front of me. So let's just drop that pretense, all right?"

The mounted guards all turned their lances toward Amra.

She smiled and twirled her sword.

"Oh, *do* make this night interesting," she said.

"Send for a truthspeaker," Ehren said, clearly desperate to keep the situation from descending into violence. "The surest way to prove the truth of both Reesa's words, and Cavan's."

"There are no priests of Zisan near Oinos," Reesa said, frowning as though her words tasted bad. "They're never allowed to pass through during the harvest. The merchants guild won't stand for it."

"Hard to respect the judgment of a place that fears truth," Amra taunted.

But Cavan had an idea.

"Sergeant." Cavan waited until he had the man's attention.

Cavan looked beyond the mace in the sergeant's hand. Saw the attentiveness and caution in his eyes. This was a man who was weighing his men's chances, if this came to a fight. And he was clever enough not to assume numbers alone would win the night.

Yes. Cavan could trust this man's honesty.

"Sergeant," Cavan said again, to emphasize the man's rank before he continued, "I assume the Council Speaker has the right of town justice. Does he have the right of king's justice?"

"Of course not," Draig answered, "but—"

"I am asking the sergeant."

"And he will answer what I allow." Draig raised an eyebrow. But before he could say whatever he next intended, Reesa spoke.

"Father has the right of town justice only. Not king's justice, nor county justice, nor baronial justice."

Draig's mouth tightened into a line and his eyes promised pain, but he did not deny his daughter's words.

"I thought as much," Cavan said with a slow smile and his eyes on Draig. "You don't possess the *authority* to charge me with espionage against Oinos. Much less try me for it. The best you could do would be to petition—"

"*Very well*," Draig said, dropping from his saddle.

"Hah!" Amra said. "Outmaneuvered him on his own battlefield. My headache is fading."

But Draig focused all of his rage on Cavan.

"You, Cavan Oltblood, have seduced my daughter, ruined the match I arranged for her, and dishonored my family. I demand satisfaction, and you cannot deny that I have the standing I need for *that*."

"Now we're talking," Amra said. She had more to say, but Qalas hushed her.

"Oh, very well," Cavan said, though his heart wasn't in it. "I assume first blood will be sufficient?"

"No," Draig said. "the duel shall last until one withdraws."

Technically, that could mean a duel to the death, if neither would withdraw, but Cavan didn't believe it would come to that.

A man like Draig put too high a value on his life to lose it in a duel.

"Fine." Cavan shrugged, drawing his *licha* sword and ensuring its reddish-yellow coloring showed in the torchlight. Long, that weapon was. Light. The dune elf forged blade had sharpness beyond anything Cavan had wielded before. Might have even rivaled Amra's sword.

"Shall we get this over with?"

"Oh, no," Draig said with an evil smile. "You shall face my champion in the town square at first light."

"And your champion shall face his," Reesa thundered, turning to face her father. "It was *I* who seduced *him*, Father. And I shall defend my actions myself."

Draig paled, but looked past her at Cavan. "Surely you need not hide behind the skirts of a girl."

"Watch that," Amra said in a warning tone, but Cavan was looking at Reesa, who pleaded silently for his agreement.

"I'm sorry," Cavan said, then turned his eyes to Draig and sheathed his blade as he finished, "but it seems I'm having trouble refusing your daughter tonight. I guess your champion shall face mine."

CAVAN DIDN'T SLEEP THAT NIGHT.

He had a big feather bed in his private room in the inn, as well as a private bathtub. He'd paid extra for such amenities, as he always did when he had the coin.

But that soft bed still carried the apples-and-honey scent of Reesa.

Reesa, who would be fighting Cavan's duel come morning.

Well...

Was it really fair for Cavan to call it *his* duel? One way to look at the situation might be to suggest that Reesa had gone to the feast that night looking for a way out of the engagement she hadn't wanted. She'd even lied, when Cavan had asked if she was promised to anyone.

From that point of view, she had dragged Cavan into this duel.

Still. Cavan had been quick enough to enjoy the company of a beauty like Reesa. He hadn't needed much seducing. What was more, Cavan *had* been the one challenged. And he didn't like letting anyone fight in his stead.

For his own part, Cavan had certainly told Reesa nothing of his own parentage and future. The gods knew he didn't like to think about those things, much less talk about them, though it seemed he had less and less choice in the matter as time had gone on.

It was not so long ago he'd managed to all but forget about the barony he'd stood to inherit — and at the time, Juno *was* a barony — until his uncle, Duke Falstaff of Nolarr, had sent hunters to kill Cavan as part of an attempt to usurp Juno and the mines that produced gemstones of powerful magic.

Cavan even fought a duel against his uncle to stop the man's ambitions, but Falstaff had found a way around his loss and an excuse to send his armies to try to claim the mines.

Cavan had gotten to the mines first and foiled Falstaff a second time, ruining the magic of those gemstones in the process. And that time King Draven made Falstaff pay for his misdeeds — in land. Enough land to turn Juno from a barony to a county.

Hells, that was half the reason Cavan and his friends were on the road now.

Yes, they were heading north to the Dragon Spike Mountains, to find a dwarven smith Cavan knew who could forge a better weapon for Qalas than the halberd he carried.

But really, Cavan wanted to set his mind on adventure once more. Leave politics for his later years, when King Draven finally passed from this world, and Cavan had no choice but to assume his duties as Count Juno.

That thought brought Cavan as close to a smile as he came that night, tossing and turning in his bed. "May he live a thousand years" was the common Oltoss way of praising the king.

In Cavan's case, he would have been only too happy to see the king live a thousand years.

Of course, the possibility existed that the king might force stewardship on Cavan if the current steward, Kent the Jeweler, the man who fostered Cavan, were to pass from this world.

So Cavan hoped Kent lived a thousand years as well. Though that wish was as much out of Cavan's love for Kent as it was out of Cavan's love for adventure.

Adventure.

Reesa had spoken of adventures. Of wishing to see the wider world. Of wishing to ride with Cavan and his friends.

If she won the duel, could Cavan refuse her? Should he?

Certainly he would owe his champion something. Still, the roads Cavan and his friends rode were dangerous. Each of them had been near death more times than Cavan liked to think about.

Reesa looked comfortable on horseback. She claimed to be good with a bow.

But would that be enough?

Was it even a question worth worrying about?

After all, if she lost the duel, she wouldn't be in a position to...

No.

Cavan sat up in his bed.

If Reesa lost her duel, Cavan could not just leave her here at the mercies of a man like Draig. Taking her on the road might not be a good option, but Cavan could at least see her safely to another town. Perhaps to relatives of her choosing.

But what if she won?

What would that mean?

Cavan gave up his attempts to sleep then. He dressed — his older, brown tunic replacing the missing good, red one — left a note for his friends that probably wasn't necessary, and spent the rest of the hours of darkness wandering the cobbled streets of Drien.

Walking was always a good way for Cavan to deal with an excess of thoughts. And besides, whatever happened in the morning, Cavan had the feeling that he'd be happy he knew the fastest ways out of town.

2

———

When dawn finally crested the titanic trees of the Wailing Woods to the east, Cavan was already at the town square. A wide area, that Cavan suspected had once been the market square. The construction in the area here looked older. Mostly fine older houses, several of them even two stories tall, unlike much of the town. And among the houses, a selection of higher end merchants such as the most fashionable tailors and jewelers in Drien.

Anchoring the town square was an impressive, three story manse that likely housed the Speaker of the Council.

Of course, considering the size of the place, it could have housed the whole of the Council of Drien, and their families. As well as whatever town business might need a great hall.

A small crowd had begun to gather, likely because the town watch had formed a large ring where the duel would take place.

Or perhaps the town watch had gossiped in the early hours of the morning. Certainly Draig hadn't sent the town criers to spread word of the duel. Most of the town would have been here by now.

Instead, Amra, Ehren and Qalas had no trouble approaching where Cavan stood, at the edge of the ring of watchmen on the far side from the manse.

Approaching on foot.

"Where are the horses?" Cavan asked.

"What did I say last night?" Amra replied, smirking at Cavan. "Not until Caramel is reshod."

"But—"

"Peace," Ehren said, offering Cavan a hunk of sausage, still warm from the inn. "If your Reesa wins this duel, we won't need to spirit her away. She'll have at least some self-determination."

"I'm not sure about that," Qalas muttered.

"And she might still need some healing that would preclude whatever quick getaway you imagine," Ehren continued, ignoring Qalas' point. "And if she loses, she'll definitely need healing. Depending on how much, she might not be able to ride before the morrow."

Ehren was the most accomplished healer Cavan knew, thanks to the blessings of Zatafa, but there were wounds that even Ehren could only heal by the first rays of a new day.

First rays that were already spending themselves when Draig and his entourage arrived.

It seemed the entire Council of Drien would bear witness to this duel, though Draig looked displeased about it. He stared daggers at Cavan, with a sour turn to his mouth and bags under his eyes that made Cavan doubt Draig had slept either.

The Council included a dozen more men and women, all human, pale skinned, and old enough for their shares of wrinkles and gray hair. A few looked to have been warriors in their youth, but most had the look of merchants, tradesmen, and farmers.

The Council had an honor guard that looked more dangerous than the town watch in general. They looked like men and women who could have chased Cavan through the streets last night without puffing for breath.

Reesa arrived with the entourage, but walked separately, and refused to even look at her father or his fellows on the Council. The crowd began buzzing at the sight of her, dressed to fight.

For good reason. Reesa this morning almost looked a warrior. She wore a long, leather jerkin, sewn throughout with rings of metal. The same kind the town watch wore.

The jerkin looked too long, and too broad on her. No doubt she'd borrowed it. She wore good leather boots, though, that covered her to the knee. They'd provide at least some protection from a low strike.

Her lovely blond hair was bound at the base of her skull so she could wear a simple steel helm that protected most of her head. Not her face, though, save for a small nose guard.

She wore a pair of short swords at her belt, and kept her hands on their pommels as she walked.

The sword belt looked well-worn, and fit properly. Cavan suspected it might have been hers. She might even have had some training with those twin short swords.

But her walk gave away her inexperience. She did not show any of last night's grace now. Her steps were slow. Cautious. Worried, perhaps. But worst of all, she was too much in her thoughts and not enough in her body. That could prove fatal in a fight.

"Reesa," Cavan called above the rising noise of the crowd. "Over here."

She shot Cavan a smile somewhere between grateful and nervous, but sped her steps to join him at the foot of the ring.

The head of the ring, of course, was where Draig and his Council stood.

And the venom in Draig's eyes turned downright poisonous. Cavan found himself glad that the man showed no talent for magic.

Of course, the township did have a wizard, somewhere. Certainly no one on or near the Council had a practitioner's aura of power...

"Lovely morning, isn't it?" Reesa asked, her voice high and tight.

"Hush," Amra said, and immediately began adjusting Reesa's armor. Tightening where she could, in ways that would make it less likely to interfere with her movement. "Have you ever used those kitchen knives before?"

"They're proper swords," Reesa said, affronted. "And I've trained with them in secret since I was a girl."

"If you think those are swords," Amra said wryly, "then you must think Cavan's packing a—"

"Have you ever used them in earnest?" Cavan asked. "Ever fought for your life?"

Reesa swallowed and shook her head.

"Keep moving," Amra said, her voice serious now. "Once the duel begins, don't stop moving. You're light and quick. I saw you dancing. Think of this as a dance too."

"Look there," Cavan said, pointing to a spot where the cobblestones were larger. "Most of the cobbles around here are fairly even, but not there. They dip smaller. If you're careful, you might get your foe to miss a step. Create an opening."

Reesa bit her lip, but noted the spot Cavan mentioned while Amra ran her through a quick drill of technique: grip, footwork, common openings and parries.

"Do you know who your opponent will be?" Ehren asked.

"Kolsach, the town champion. By law, he's the only one who *can* serve as my father's champion."

Drums. Cavan didn't see them, but he heard them.

"That would be him now," Reesa said, and she paled.

Cavan could understand why.

Kolsach was a name Cavan recognized. The man had been a mercenary captain for two or three different companies over the course of about two decades.

Rumor had it that he was still every bit as tough and strong as he'd ever been.

He certainly looked it, now that Cavan could see him.

The man stood tall. Even taller than Cavan, by about a handspan. Well-muscled, though much of the leanness of youth seemed to have fled him now. His belly had grown beyond that of the man the stories portrayed.

But Cavan would have recognized the crossed scars on the man's left cheek anywhere. No one else was said to have them, or at least none so jagged. And he had a dangerous look to his eyes.

Kolsach wore a chain hauberk with sleeves, and leggings to

match, tucked into heavy, calf-high boots. No helm for him, though. His long brown hair was tied back in a braid behind his head.

And he didn't carry a sword. He carried the weapon that Kolsach had made himself famous for using. Siegebreaker: a huge warhammer. Blunted on the top, squared on one side and a spike on the reverse.

Amra tutted. Smacked Reesa's jerkin. "You knew you were facing a man who fights with a warhammer and you wore this? Are you clothed beneath it?"

Reesa nodded, her eyes still on Kolsach.

"Come on then," Amra said, hurrying to get the leather jerkin off of Reesa. "Won't do you much good against that thing, and it'll slow you down. Especially since you're obviously not used to wearing it."

Underneath the leather jerkin, Reesa wore Cavan's red tunic. The one he'd worn to the feast. Left behind in his rush last night. A sight that made him smile. The tunic was too big for her, but with the sleeves pinned high and the torso bound at her waist by her sword belt, it wouldn't hinder her as that jerkin would have.

"He can swing that thing fast, but it's beastly heavy," Amra advised Reesa, quietly. "Keep moving and you may get him off-balance. Stop moving and you're an easy target."

"Cavan Oltblood," Draig called out. "This is your last opportunity to be a man and fight to defend your own honor. Do not hide behind—"

"If you don't think women can fight, Draig," Amra bellowed in her command voice, and Cavan could practically hear the warning flutter of her eyelashes, "I'll be more than happy to give you a personal lesson right here in front of everyone."

"Behind *my daughter*," Draig said, refusing to look at Amra, or even away from Cavan. "This is our fight. Let it be done properly."

"This is *my* fight," Reesa said, steel coming into her voice once more. "It was *I* who seduced *him*, Father. As I told you last night." Reesa gave the crowd a moment to recover from that proclamation before continuing. "If you feel that my deed dishonored the family, then it is only right that I defend my actions."

"Reesa—" Draig started, but Reesa drew her swords and clashed them together up high to drown out his objection.

She spoke louder then, loud enough for the whole crowd to hear, voice brimming with righteous anger.

"But I am still your daughter, and I cannot take up arms against my own father. If you will fight for yourself, then I will have no choice but to let Cavan fight this duel. As he is eager to do."

Cavan let his lips stretch in a wicked smile. "More than eager."

"You know the town law forbids it," Draig replied.

"The whole of the Council of Drien is here to witness," Reesa continued, "and these are unusual circumstances. If they vote here and now to allow their Speaker the honor of fighting for himself in this single instance, then you cannot hide behind the law."

"It is not proper for me to fight a duel," Draig said. "And I have no need to ask, to know that the Council feels the same way."

Cavan thought that a few members of the Council might have disagreed, to judge by a few sour expressions, but said nothing.

"The law makes clear that the town champion must fight any challenges involving the Speaker, or any of the Council," Draig continued. "But there is no reason to risk yourself in this fight, Reesa. Set down your swords. Give up your dreams of action and adventure, and be the proper daughter you were raised to be. We may still find a good life for you."

"If you will not fight for yourself," Reesa said, "then with Cavan's permission, I shall defend the actions that I initiated."

Reesa looked at Cavan, and this time there was no question in her look. She was *demanding* that Cavan allow her to fight this duel.

Cavan hated sending her against a foe like Kolsach, but he nodded.

"I like her," Amra said. "Can't say I think much of her taste in men, but she does have spirit."

"You mean you and Cavan never..." Qalas let the question trail off.

"Please," Amra said. "He's got some muscle, but he's too skinny for me. I like my men with more power to their build. Cavan's too much a wizard and not enough a warrior. And he has only the three scars."

"The one below his collarbone *is* impressive though," Ehren said.

"Granted, but—"

The drums sounded again.

"A kiss for your champion?" Reesa asked, tension raising her pitch again. Sweat already beaded on her forehead, despite the cool of the morning air.

"Of course," Cavan said, and he gave her the only present he could offer.

A deep and meaningful kiss.

Reesa dropped her swords and clutched Cavan as though worried that this might be the final kiss of her life. So if it were, Cavan did his best to make that kiss a good one.

Ehren stepped into the circle and repeated his morning prayers aloud for the crowd, in the tongue of ancient Penthix. Morning prayers that the priest had already made by the first rays of dawn, as he did every day.

Whether Ehren did that because he knew Drien to revere Zatafa, or to give Cavan and Reesa a little more time, Cavan could not have guessed. But either way, he was grateful.

As Ehren's final prayed ended with a dramatic crescendo, the drums sounded once more.

It was time for the duel to begin.

Cavan's whole nervous system felt as though it were trying to fight the duel for Reesa. Or perhaps had fought a dozen duels already, by the early light of the late summer morning.

His heart was pounding, and his stomach felt as though it might reject that breakfast sausage Ehren had brought him from the inn.

The sun was still rising, and the sky still orange and red, as Reesa and Kolsach took their assigned places, a good dozen paces apart within the circle set by the town watch.

Kolsach frowned as though he considered this duel beneath him.

Or perhaps he found it distasteful to duel with Reesa. Or perhaps he did not think she would offer him enough sport.

Or perhaps there was some other cause. Cavan simply didn't know the man. Still. Cavan had trouble ascribing nobility to the ex-mercenary.

Among the crowd, vendors had already begun to circulate, offering ales and selections of roast meats for those who had not yet broken their fasts.

Kolsach twirled his hammer in a complicated form of salute.

Reesa clashed her twin swords above her head in her own salute.

Draig was talking to the Council, but they were all shaking their heads.

"A moment," Draig called, and accompanied whatever he said now with significant gestures.

A wrinkled, silver-haired woman on the Council stepped forward. Cavan could almost hear her words, sharp and high and a little creaky, but firm enough.

Whatever reply Draig hoped to hear, he wasn't getting it.

The crowd had already begun chanting for their favorites. And though the chants for Kolsach were strong, Cavan was pleased at the number of people chanting Reesa's name.

Though a number of those people shot dirty looks at Cavan, as though he'd been afraid to fight Kolsach.

"Enough delays," Kolsach bellowed. "For the honor of Drien, let us begin!"

Draig tried to yell something, but whatever he would have said was drowned out by the roar of the crowd.

Cavan tried to join in chanting for Reesa, but his nerves were against it. Especially with Amra and Qalas discussing the duel as it took place.

Kolsach leapt forward, bringing his warhammer around in a mighty swing, low enough to sweep Reesa's legs out from under her.

But Reesa was nimble. She leapt over the blow. Slashed out at Kolsach with both blades.

Alas, her swords only bounced off the mail of his chest.

But then she was behind him. Twirling and bringing both swords around again in a unified strike.

This time her blades were blocked by the handle of Kolsach's hammer.

"I thought it was too much to hope the handle was all wood," Amra said.

"Are you kidding?" Qalas said. "A handle that long for a hammer that heavy, it needs more support than most woods can give."

"Of course, this close to the Wailing Woods," Amra countered, "it could be all wood. If forest elves supplied it. Those trees are something else."

Cavan stepped away from the banter of his friends. Kept his focus on the dodging and weaving of Reesa. She kept herself a step or two ahead of that warhammer, but the blows were coming too close for Cavan's comfort.

"One shot from that thing and it's over," he muttered. Kolsach was simply too strong. And he kept that warhammer moving all too fast.

"If so," Ehren said, keeping his voice quiet, "I'll make sure she's not crippled for life. Don't worry."

"If her father allows you to heal her. He seems the type to use this to teach her a lesson."

Before Ehren could reply, the crowd oohed.

Kolsach shifted the angle of a swing at the last instant. Caught one of Reesa's ankles.

Fortunately, she was in the air at the time, attempting to leap again over that deadly warhammer. So at least some of the blow was mitigated.

Still, the force of the swing spun her and threw her to the cobblestones. She landed with a grunt of pain, but she didn't act as though it were the first time she were ever struck.

Already she gathered herself.

"Well named," Ehren muttered, which reminded Cavan that Reesa was the name of an ancient Rentissi warrior queen.

"I hope you're right," Cavan whispered back.

Kolsach came in with his weapon's handle, stabbing downward at the prone woman.

Reesa rolled aside. Swung her own swords with all the force she could muster from the ground.

Not much, but enough. Cavan saw Kolsach wince as both blades slammed against the mail coating his right forearm, one and then the other, no more than two finger-widths apart.

Kolsach was right-handed. Those blows might slow his attacks a little, if she were lucky.

Cavan hoped Reesa's luck was better than his own. He bit the inside of his cheek, as though what good luck he had could be transferred to her.

Reesa was back on her feet now, but clearly favoring her hurt left foot. Uncertainty in her eyes.

Kolsach saw that. Grinned as though his triumph were at hand. Spoke to her, in a low voice. Taunts, to judge from his expression.

Whatever he said, Reesa didn't like it. The fear on her face was replaced by the fury Cavan had seen the night before, when she'd turned on her father. And she spat words of her own right back at Kolsach.

The next strike came in high. Reesa had no trouble ducking under it. More than that, she used the momentum. Swung the sword in her right hand. Aiming for the same place she'd hit his arm before.

The mail might have kept her blades from cutting his arm off, but they wouldn't stop the shock of the blow. No doubt he would have bruises from her efforts, once the fight was done.

But her blows were not solid enough to stop muscles like Kolsach's, unfortunately. He winced at the strike, but his control of the mighty warhammer seemed just as sure as it had before.

He started pacing around her. Making her limp in place, turning to face him.

"She needs to keep moving," Amra said, frowning. "Even if it hurts."

"Perhaps she's saving her ankle for a desperate move," Qalas suggested.

"If so, she'd better do it soon."

Kolsach feinted twice, then thrust forward with the mallet of his hammer. The feints had thrown Reesa's balance off, and the thrust was too unexpected for her, inexperienced as she was.

The blow struck her ribs solidly. Drove her back. She fell backward into a roll that took her clear of Kolsach's follow-up, a swing that might have taken her life.

Cavan didn't like the change in Kolsach's demeanor. His movements. The man looked to be treating this as a duel to the death now.

Whatever the two had discussed there in the center of the dueling ring, Kolsach had clearly been infuriated by Reesa's words.

Reesa found her feet again in time to dive to her left and somersaulted to avoid another blow. Impressive, the way she could handle twin short swords through rolls and somersaults.

But Kolsach was pressing harder now.

"That's it," Amra said, voice low and tense. "Keep him moving. You've gotten in his head. Use it, girl, use it."

"Do you really think she has?" Qalas asked, but Amra was too focused on the way Reesa kept diving, rolling and spinning to answer.

But that blow to the chest she'd taken. Every roll made her grimace in pain. And already her face had gone white as first frost.

Cavan had to hope Amra was right. And that Reesa would figure out how to turn Kolsach's rage to her advantage.

Soon.

Kolsach's swings were getting wilder now. Taking him more off balance each time. He clearly had no fear of a counterattack, and wanted a decisive blow.

The crowd's chanting swelled. More and more seeming to want the fight over, even if agreement wasn't universal about who should win.

Kolsach seemed to be speaking as he kept swinging. But Cavan couldn't see Reesa's face from his angle. Had no way to know if she taunted the ex-mercenary right back, or merely held her tongue and kept moving.

But then it happened.

Reesa somersaulted right past the spot Cavan had pointed out to her. The spot where the cobblestones were most uneven.

Kolsach was too fixated on his own rage to notice the dip.

He came in hard with a swing, but he got his footing wrong. He went down just as Reesa hobbled to her feet.

She had one opportunity as he started to rise.

She took it.

Reesa brought the flats of both her blades hard against Kolsach's unprotected face, one from each side.

Kolsach, stunned, could only teeter and shake his head as Reesa hopped one-footed to stand behind him.

He could scarcely move, save a reflexive raising of his warhammer.

But the move was automatic. And too late to stop the next blows.

Reesa slammed the flats of both blades against the soft spot at the base of Kolsach's skull. One right after the other.

He went down like a felled tree.

Reesa quickly kicked the warhammer away from him. Then swore loud enough to be heard clear across the Dwarfmarches and fell to the cobblestones, because she'd kicked with the wrong foot.

She used the hilts of her swords to help herself back to a standing position.

Kolsach stirred. Tried to raise his head. A slow movement. Unsteady. He tried to shake his head and winced.

Hopping on one foot now, she stood over Kolsach, between him and his warhammer. Put both her blades against his throat.

The crowd grew quiet. Not even chanting her name now.

Cavan heard her next words.

"Yield or die."

Kolsach glared at her. Looked to be gauging the distance to her ankles.

Reesa pressed the edges of her swords tighter, pinning his head to the cobblestones, and drawing dripping red lines on both sides of his throat.

"I say again. Yield or die."

Kolsach dropped his head in defeat.

"I yield!"

***

FOR A MOMENT, THE WHOLE OF THE TOWN SQUARE SEEMED FROZEN IN place. The crowd surrounding the just-ended duel. The ring of town watchmen, holding them back. The Council of Drien at the head of the circle.

Even Cavan and his friends, at the foot of the circle.

But Master Powys had always said, *Time is a tool. It must serve the wizard, or the wizard will serve it.*

Cavan might have failed his apprenticeship to that great wizard. But that did not mean he'd failed all his lessons.

So even in that seemingly frozen moment, Cavan was able to perceive the whole of the world around him.

The morning breeze, gentle now, but showing signs that it would grow strong by noon and bring rain clouds by evening.

The glistening gold of early morning sun, in a sky still prying its daily blue from the purples of night through their war of orange.

The wrest birds singing their eight-note trills. Their small black-feathered bodies circling in hope of blood, or at least the trash left by the crowd when it departed.

Draig. The old man torn between emotions Cavan could not quite parse. But he looked to be settling on anger.

The Council surrounding Draig. Most with faces schooled to show no reactions at all — those who had spent their youths as farmers, tradesmen, and merchants, mainly — and several with eyes flaring with triumph. Though whether they celebrated Reesa's victory over Kolsach, or a loss of honor for Draig at the defeat of his champion, Cavan could not guess.

Cavan noted an older woman on the Council, standing to one side, who looked thoroughly upset about the turn of events. He noted her graying chestnut hair and slender, elegant build, and most of all the short, single scar on the left side of her chin. She dressed in breeches and tunic, with a slender sword of her own at her hip.

That woman only looked away from Kolsach to stare hatred at Reesa.

Kolsach lay limp on the ground, not bothering to try to rise just yet.

And Reesa. No triumph in her expression, but Cavan understood. Triumph would likely come later. For now, only dull unreality and a grimace of pain.

It was Reesa who broke that frozen moment.

She collapsed.

Cavan was past the town watch before they could think to try to stop him. Amra right beside him. Ehren hot on their heels, and Qalas a few steps behind.

The crowd roared, cheering the victor and seemingly unconcerned that she'd collapsed.

Cavan reached for Reesa, but Ehren interposed his goldenwood staff.

"Do not move her until I say," Ehren said, checking Reesa's eyes and nodding to himself.

Reesa blinked, frowned. Tried to speak, and winced.

Amra collected the fallen short swords.

"With your permission," Ehren said, and when Reesa nodded, he quickly and tenderly checked her ribs and her ankle.

"Shouldn't be too bad," Amra said, "she dodges well."

"Foot's bad," Ehren said, already pulling bandages and herbs from his seemingly bottomless leather backpack. "Ribs are bruised, front and back. Think you avoided getting them cracked. But that foot has at least two broken bones."

But Ehren nodded at Cavan, and Cavan knelt and drew Reesa's head onto his lap. He pulled the helmet off to stroke her sweat-dampened hair.

"Knew you were a good dancer," Cavan said with a lopsided smile, trying to distract Reesa while Ehren set about his work, beginning with unlacing her boot.

Reesa tried to smile, but it came out a grimace.

"That is *my* daughter!"

Draig's voice, over the hubbub of the crowd, which even now the town watch was dispersing.

"And I'm sure she's proud of that," Amra said, turning to face the Speaker, "even if I wouldn't be. But what she needs right now is a healer, not a lecture."

Cavan looked up to see Draig surrounded by his hard-looking personal guard. Those were definitely men who'd survived their share of battles and had the scars to prove it.

No wonder Amra was taunting.

Reesa grabbed both Cavan's hands and squeezed.

Draig's voice sounded tight enough to snap, when he responded.

"While I'm sure that this priest of Zatafa here has the best of intentions, his efforts are not needed. My daughter's wounds will be treated by our house priest, and she will convalesce in the privacy of her own home. Now all of you, *step aside.*"

"Reesa?" Amra called without looking away from Draig. "You want to go with Daddy? Or do you want Cavan's best friend to heal you?"

"The choice is not hers to make," Draig said, even as Reesa said, "I am honored to be treated by Ehren."

Cavan looked for that town watch sergeant from last night, but saw only Draig's personal guards standing nearby. A half dozen of them, in oiled chainmail, hands ready on the pommels of their broadswords.

Qalas seemed to have noted that as well. He'd subtly shifted his footing, as well as his grip on his halberd.

"Reesa," Cavan said softly, "I think I better stand."

Reesa's brow looked troubled, but she nodded and released Cavan's hands.

He eased her head down onto her helm, and stood.

"Ah, the coward himself," Draig said.

"I'm pretty sure my honor came out of that duel all right," Cavan said with a shrug. "How about yours, Draig? Seems to me you were going to lose either way."

"I want you all out of my town by midday," Draig said. "If any of you are still here past the apex of Zatafa's glory, I swear I will make you regret it. And I can."

Amra drew breath to speak, but Cavan got words out first.

"Only too happy to oblige," Cavan said, with a slight bow that could only be taken as mockery. "Ehren, will Reesa be able to ride by afternoon? Or will we require a cart?"

"Oh, not a cart," Amra said. "We'll be *forever* getting anywhere."

"Cart *would* be better," Ehren said, "but I can speed things up if we need to."

He started digging in his backpack.

Draig gave Cavan an oily smile.

"You seem to be laboring under the misapprehension that my daughter will be accompanying you. She will not."

"Reesa," Cavan said, without looking away from Draig. "Last night you said you craved to see the world beyond the borders of this town. And as you defended my honor today, it seems the very least I could do for you would be to escort you on the road to somewhere more to your liking. Would you care to ride with us when we leave today?"

"I can think of *nothing* I want more."

That Amra did not reply to that sentence with innuendo was a fact that Cavan could only interpret as meaning she expected a fight. He noticed she'd shifted her grip on Reesa's short swords, so the blades lay flat along her forearms.

Cavan smelled the distinctive scent of an orange being peeled. That meant that Ehren considered the situation important enough to use one of his blessed oranges, which would speed Reesa's healing dramatically.

"I believe the matter is settled," Cavan said.

"I assure you," Draig said, "it is not."

Draig nodded to his guards.

Looked as though, once more, Amra was right.

SIX HARDENED GUARDS, SPREADING OUT IN THE EARLY MORNING LIGHT. The cobblestones of the town square all but empty now, save for the two groups: Draig and his guards, and Cavan and his friends.

Strange that the rest of the Council of Drien vanished so quickly. But then, Kolsach was gone as well. And Cavan had no time to worry about any of them right then.

More concerning was that the town watch, after busily clearing away the crowd from the duel, seemed content to have gone back to their duties. Which apparently did not involve stopping this little dispute.

Then again, members of the watch had to live in this town. Cavan had the impression that Draig enjoyed making life difficult for those who interfered with his wishes.

Draig would wait though. His guards were more important, just at the moment.

And Cavan had noticed something.

Yes, those guards looked lean and mean and scarred. Yes, their chainmail was oiled and ready, and their broadswords looked to have seen much use.

But something about the look of those men, or maybe the way they moved, suggested to Cavan that their scars were *old* scars. That maybe serving as Draig's personal guard meant few opportunities for real action.

That maybe it had been some time since those guards had seen the kind of challenges warriors needed to keep their skills as sharp as their swords. After all, training could go only so far.

Interesting...

All six of Draig's guards started to pull their swords.

"No!" Ehren cried out. "We have a wounded woman right here, and she's not ready to move. Do you want to step on her?"

"He has a point," Cavan said, not yet drawing his own sword.

Amra, Cavan noticed, had not dropped Reesa's short swords nor gone for her own two-handed blade. She might have been letting

Cavan take the lead here, or she might have had a plan. Hard to be sure which.

Could have been both, knowing her.

Qalas simply adjusted his grip on his halberd. He had a ready look in his eyes.

"Ehren is right," Cavan said to Draig, ignoring the now-drawn blades of the guards and focusing on their master. "We start a fight right here, you know someone might step on your daughter. Or fall on her. Or bleed on her. Just how much risk do you want to put her to this morning?"

"She risks herself," Draig said. "She's disobeyed me at every turn."

"Father!" Reesa said, and her voice sounded stronger, less tight than it had before Ehren had given her one of those miraculous healing oranges.

"You have defied me before the whole of Drien. You wish to ride with these *wanderers*? Then you can fall with them."

Draig turned away.

The first of the guards started to raise his sword.

Before that blade had moved a fingerspan, Amra was already in motion.

She dove between two guards, thrusting Reesa's short swords into the slight gaps under their belts, between those guards' hauberks and leggings. Straight into the flesh underneath.

And Amra left the swords in her wake, as those guards went down, screaming.

Qalas followed Amra's movement, only a fraction of a beat behind. He stabbed at the nearest guard with the tip of his halberd. Enough strength behind the thrust that the guard had to sidestep as well as parry to keep himself unstabbed.

But Qalas whirled with the parry.

The guard lunged for what he thought was an opening. But his sword was too far out of line. His blow a little too slow.

Qalas struck while still spinning. All his momentum and strength working together. He slammed the steel-wrapped handle of his halberd across his foe's head.

That guard went down, and just like that, there were three.

Cavan stepped away from Reesa. Drew his sword. Slowly. Made a point of it.

Amra drew her own sword at the same pace. The same synchronicity of movements and sounds. Amra's and Cavan's own little way of reminding these guards just how many times they'd fought side-by-side.

Not to mention how recently.

Qalas could not quite match the movement or sound with his halberd, but he made a show of raising it in the same moment, bringing the axe head to menace another guard.

The two guards on the ground continued to cry out in pain.

"That's half your number," Cavan said simply, "and we haven't even begun. Her sword and mine? We'll cut through that mail like you were naked."

Cavan tilted his sword to show the orange and red swirls along the blade, trusting that experienced warriors would recognize the dune elf metal.

"So," Cavan said. "Are you sure you wish to meet your gods today?"

"Every man meets the gods when they call for him," one of the guards answered. Apparently the leader. Certainly, he had the most scars. Three on his face alone, and another on his neck that dipped down past his collar. "And now that you've stepped away from the Speaker's daughter—"

That guard leapt at Cavan, sword high and ready.

Cavan slipped past the attack, while metal rang out as the remaining guards tried their luck with Amra and Qalas.

Amra's screamed and fell before Cavan even had time to finish his first strike.

Cavan's guard was quick, and skilled. He had his sword up for a parry that should have set up a counterattack. But his steel, while decent, could not stand against *licha*. Sparks danced and spat as the steel broadsword groaned and lost some of its blade.

The guard might have known what *licha* was, but he'd clearly never seen it in action before. He lost a critical moment, eyes flicking in surprise at the sight of the sparks shooting off his blade. Wincing at the heat of those shavings bouncing off his skin.

Cavan took that moment. Slipped in close. Slammed the hilt of his sword against the man's temple, and dropped him to the cobblestones.

"He does take forever in a fight, doesn't he?" Qalas said to Amra, almost matching her smirk.

"Well, he's only half a warrior, remember," Amra said. "If Ehren hadn't lectured him and *lectured* him about how spells are illegal in this town, no doubt he would have just thrown a spell and brought his guard down as fast as ... well ... faster than he *did*, anyway."

All six of Draig's guards were on the ground now. Four were bleeding, wounded badly, and two were at least unconscious from blows to the head.

"I suggest you call that healer of yours," Cavan said to the open-mouthed Draig. "All of these men might yet live, and our friend Ehren is a touch busy right now."

"Help!" Draig yelled out, drawing his sword but making no move to fight. "Town watch! These people just butchered my guards and threatened my life."

Amra gave Cavan a significant look as they could hear someone echo that cry.

"Ehren," Cavan said, "can she—"

"No, you'll have to carry her."

Cavan sheathed his sword and scooped up Reesa while Amra collected Reesa's short swords.

And they all took off running for their inn.

"I told you to bring the horses," Cavan grumbled.

Cavan expected to be bringing up the rear on the run back to the inn, but he didn't.

Amra was out front, Reesa's short swords in her hands, but the blades tucked against her forearms to avoid seeming a threat. No doubt her eyes scanning for danger.

Qalas was right behind her, halberd up and ready, but not threatening anyone just at the moment.

Cavan came third in their little parade, cradling Reesa in his arms. Reesa, for her part, looked irritated that she had to be carried. But she did not struggle. She clung to Cavan, perhaps trying to lighten her own weight.

Ehren followed last, as much to keep rear guard as to keep an eye on his patient.

The hue and cry from the town watch came slower than Cavan expected — perhaps because of how quickly they cleared the town square for Draig's little attempted murder — but it did come.

And watchmen were following all too soon.

Fortunately, Cavan and his friends ran well enough that they were able to keep just ahead of the hue and cry. They were able to keep at least a small lead on their pursuers.

Unfortunately, even that lead would only last until they reached the inn.

And they were almost there.

The inn in question was Mountainfall, one of the few two-story buildings on its block, with its own stables in the back, and entirely too much open space around it.

As with all the streets in this town, no two buildings were built close together. Cavan had never seen a town so obsessed with open space, and right now it would only cause more problems for him.

"Ready the horses," Ehren called. "I'll throw down our things."

But before he could head for the solid wooden front door under the sign of rocks falling down a mountainside, mist rose up as though from the ground itself.

"Cavan?" Amra called quickly, drawing her sword.

"Not mine," Cavan said, as the mist rose swiftly, obscuring all sight.

He knew the spell. Had used it many times himself. Wished he'd cast it right then, so he could have opened his own eyes, and those of his friends, to that mist so that it would not prove a barrier.

"The mist is mine." The voice came over from where Cavan knew the stables to be. It was a woman's voice tempered with maturity, but still full of strength.

"Maran?" Reesa asked.

"Here, child."

"It's safe," Reesa said. "The town wizard is an old friend."

A tunnel opened in the mist, leading the way to the stables. A tunnel that closed behind Cavan and his friends as they followed it.

Now *that* was a trick Cavan couldn't have accomplished.

Amra and Qalas led the way, weapons ready, but Cavan and Ehren stayed only a step behind.

If Cavan had not noticed her fairly impressive aura of power, he might have mistaken Maran for an innkeeper. She had that kind of matronly look, as of a woman who enjoyed life, and let it enjoy her.

She stood scarcely tall enough to reach the center of Cavan's chest, and she wore robes of rich red velvet. She had graying chestnut hair that fell in a braid over her right shoulder. Her reddened cheeks dimpled as she smiled at Reesa.

Amra and Qalas stepped past Maran to ready the horses, leaving the wizard for Cavan to deal with.

"I trust," Maran said before Cavan could speak, "you'll forgive me for having your horses readied. I suspected there might be a hasty exit after the duel."

Surest sign of a full wizard, Cavan thought with a touch of self-deprecation. *Always two moves ahead.*

"There's a fifth horse tacked and ready," Qalas called out. "A black mare courser. Young."

"Horizon?" Reesa said, her whole expression filling with hope.

The mare whinnied in response.

Cavan could hear shouts from the streets. Some saying the murderers had fled one direction, some claiming another.

"Of course," Maran said. "You cannot leave without your steed, silly girl. Much less your bow, and provisions."

Cavan carried Reesa to the black courser and helped her mount while Maran explained.

"Your father is not the worst Speaker this town has seen, but his ambition will be his end. And I won't see him take you down with him, sweet thing."

"Thank you, Maran!" Reesa said, giving the older wizard a strong hug, while Cavan mounted his blue roan hobby, Dzint. "But won't Father come after you for this?"

"Let him try. I've served this town far longer than he has, and I've faced worse than your father. Now. If the road isn't all you dream it to be," Maran said, tone full of warning, "I suggest you visit your cousins in Sarkis. Write me from there and I will help you decide your next move."

"While that's lovely and all," Amra said, from the back of her own bay hobby, Caramel — who apparently had been reshod — "I don't relish riding these cobblestones through a thick mist."

"Nor shall you," Maran said picking up a cup that rested on the edge of Horizon's stall. She muttered words of power while flicking water at each of them and their horses. Cavan couldn't hear much of the spell, but he recognized a conjugation of the verb *Zeh*, which was the verb he would have used to call a mist from the barrels of water about town.

As soon as Maran's flicked water touched Cavan, the mist seemed to vanish.

"I suggest you ride west and cross the river before turning on your way. The whole town believes you are traveling north, so Draig will position guards to the north and the south first. Leave now and you should have time to leave town safely."

"Thank you, wise one," Cavan said, addressing her as the more advanced wizard she was.

"Take care of this one, and I'll count it thanks enough," Maran said.

And then they were on the move.

Cavan led the way through the streets, having determined the fastest ways out of town during last night's wanderings.

Reesa followed, on Horizon, then Amra on Caramel. Ehren came next, on his blond chestnut hobby, Highsun. Qalas brought up the rear on his buckskin rouncey, Ondiq.

Cavan had worried for a moment that the sound of their hooves would give them away. But it seemed that Maran had thought of that as well.

No sooner were Cavan and his friends riding than he heard the sound of riders going every which way at a full gallop. What town watchmen Cavan saw looked more confused and scattered than likely to pursue.

As for the innocent townsfolk between the inn and that bridge, they were easy to spot thanks to Maran's magic, and even easier to avoid because the few that moved through the mist moved slowly.

Before long Cavan and his friends were out of town, across the bridge, and on the road again, riding between farms.

Cavan was only too happy to see Drien receding in the distance. A town where he had not gotten to fight his own battles, nor cast his own spells?

He couldn't wait to forget it.

Far as Cavan was concerned, the best part of Drien was on the horse behind him.

What he didn't know, was exactly what that meant.

3

———

THE ROAD OUT OF OINOS WAS WIDE ENOUGH THAT IT MUST HAVE SEEN A good deal of caravan traffic, and dusty enough that the summer near here must have been hot and dry.

The air was cooler now, with fall around the corner, but the rains had not not come through yet. At least, not enough to make a difference to the dusty road.

No caravans that day though. Only local traders pulling wagons by hand and heading farm to farm, or into Drien.

The road held due west for quite a distance. Far longer than Cavan and his friends stayed with it.

Ehren, of course, had been against leaving the road. But that was only out of concern for Reesa, and the discomfort she would face if they rode overland before he could mend her wounds completely, by the light of the next dawn.

Reesa refused to let her broken foot slow them down any more than it had to.

And so, as soon as they were past the farms and somewhere into the kingdom west of Oinos — Cavan was pretty sure its name was Holfast, though he couldn't remember who ruled here — they turned northwest and left the road behind.

Due north might have been the fastest way to reach the Dragon Spikes, but northwest was a more direct route to the particular dwarf Cavan had in mind to be the forger of a new weapon for Qalas. Assuming that dwarf still lived and worked where he had, when last Cavan saw him.

And assuming that Cavan remembered the lay of this part of the continent as well as he believed. He hadn't ridden this way in a number of years.

Once off the road, their concession to Reesa's condition was to give up concerns over speed. They may not have needed it anyway. From what Reesa said, Sarkis was west and south, and Maran was likely to let slip — convincingly — that Reesa would want to go that way first.

A tricky game, admitting a potential ultimate destination, but pretending it was an early destination. By the time they determined Reesa was not in Sarkis, it would probably be safe for her to go there.

Assuming that was what she wanted.

A day's riding and walking their horses (Reesa still sitting her horse as they walked, of course), and Cavan still felt no nearer to asking Reesa just what she imagined life on the road would be. Nor what she really wanted, traveling with them as she was now.

Least of all did Cavan want to ask what Reesa wanted from *him*, but that was the question he came back to most often, in his mind.

They had had only the one night together, after all. Surely she did not, as her father appeared to, imagine that she would now marry Cavan...

Though Cavan could do far worse for a bride, when that day came. Beautiful, fiery, good at dancing and riding, passably good with a sword...

Thoughts like those, and their potential answers, kept Cavan quiet on the day's ride.

The others seemed content not to press Reesa too hard as they traveled, either. Qalas, Amra and Ehren each took turns telling one story or another of their adventures.

Though, Cavan noted, they made sure that each such story demonstrated the dangers they faced in their travels.

Qalas did engage Reesa in some discussion of bows and shooting, which conversation Amra joined in as well. Cavan heard enough of this to conclude that Reesa was at least used to shooting her bow at small, moving targets such as ducks in flight and rabbits on the run.

She might be good with that bow after all.

And it seemed that Reesa was a true follower of Zatafa. Or at least, she joined in the songs Ehren sang throughout the day, and she never once complained about Ehren's singing voice.

By the time they set their camp that night, Cavan was no more ready to ask the questions he dreaded. So he made sure to focus on checking their surroundings.

They set their camp in a clearing in a small woods. Evergreens, mostly, this far north, but pale puny things beside the mighty trees Cavan had seen in the Wailing Woods.

These trees grew no wider across than the length of his arm, and their heights scarcely topped what he might see in a common guard tower. Their bark was almost light as that of birch woods.

Cavan did not know these trees. So he collected a few fallen sticks, as well as bits of bark, and a handful of the thick, sweet-smelling needle leaves.

New trees might have interesting properties, and Master Powys had taught Cavan the tricks to learning the secrets of herbs, plants, and trees.

But the area itself looked safe enough. Their clearing had not been used for camps in the last several weeks, and even in looking around he could see no recent signs of riders, nor anyone marching in numbers.

Outside of the woods here, the land was largely rolling grasslands and thickened regions of brambles and thorny undergrowth. They were away from the farmed areas, and they were still well enough short of the Dragon's Eye, the largest lake in the area, and the rivers it fed that Cavan suspected he was riding through a no man's land.

Officially it likely belonged to one kingdom or another, but unofficially no one settled here, because it was too remote from the local towns and cities to be worth the bother, and not rich enough in resources to merit expansion.

Or perhaps Holfast and its northern neighbor had warred enough times to leave a comfortable uninhabited zone between themselves. A place to drive any raiding orc tribes, perhaps.

Amra would know.

But Amra had already begun the questions.

The bedrolls were scarcely laid out in the dying light, and Ehren had only just begun to roast a brace of chickens, along with a selection of vegetables, all from that wondrous pack of his.

And yet Amra had already begun the questions. Starting with the issue Cavan considered least important, himself.

"So," Amra said, smiling at Reesa, "I've got to know. You were supposed to stay a virgin until whatever marriage your father arranged for you..."

"To Jace, eldest son of Count Vulyys," Reesa said with a grimace. "Fair enough to look at, I suppose, but the kind of noble who thinks hunting should involve him pointing at a deer, someone else killing it, and him getting the credit."

"Whatever," Amra said, waving away the description and getting on with her question. "What I want to know is, was *Jace* supposed to be a virgin too?"

"Of course," Reesa said, open surprise on her face that it was even a question. "Oinos takes a dim view of bastards among its nobility. It's considered a sign of weakness. The fashion has begun to spread among the more successful merchants. Few major families would be willing ... to ... risk..."

Reesa paled and looked at Cavan.

"That explains why we didn't meet any Oinbloods on our way through." Cavan smiled. "Fortunately for me, King Draven of Oltoss doesn't feel the same way."

"Meanwhile," Amra said, through the first strains of laughter, "the nobles of Oinoss go to their marriage bed with no idea what they're doing!"

Amra fell backward onto her bedroll, lost in peals of hilarity.

"Wait," Ehren said, looking over from the fire and talking over Amra's amusement. "Then why did your father keep emphasizing Cavan's bastardy?"

"Because I'd sullied myself, to his way of thinking," Reesa said bitterly. "Not fit for a noble of Oinos anymore, but fit enough for a bastard of Oltoss."

"How did you think he'd react?" Qalas asked, frowning.

"I wasn't really *thinking* at the time," Reesa said, making a show of looking anywhere but Cavan.

"More urgent at the moment," Ehren said, "is for us to know what you have in mind. You wished to leave Drien. Well, the whole world lies before you. Where would you go?"

"Keeping in mind," Amra said, sitting up quickly, "that we are about our own business."

"But we'll make time to see you someplace *safe*," Ehren said, aiming his sharp tone at Amra.

Reesa gave Cavan a helpless look.

"It's all right," Cavan said, then quirked a half-smile for his friends that belied the unease in his gut. "I offered you the chance to ride with us. So you can ride with us. We're heading for the Dragon Spike mountains, to see a dwarf about a halberd."

"Not exactly a safe route," Qalas said. "Lots of orc territory, and worse. And I still worry about what sort of 'favor' this friend of yours will ask to make me a weapon."

"The key is," Cavan said, "there will likely be stops at a town or two between here and there, if you wish to follow a different path. And if your goal is Sarkis, well, unless you want to go there now, we might have to see you situated safely in a more northern town for a time, until we finish our business with the dwarf."

"How long do we have, anyway?" Qalas asked. "Isn't this a marching year?"

"Yes. And since we've been passing harvest festivals, the march probably starts in no more than a week or so. But that won't matter. Ranka doesn't join the march. Says the Black Shield Mountains in the south don't produce any metals good enough for his anvil, so he won't waste his time down there."

"The orcs though. Most tribes will push east, unless they can unite enough to—"

But Amra cut Qalas off with a raised hand.

A moment later, Cavan heard the snapping of a twig.

They had company.

CAVAN HAD BEEN FACING THE FIRE BEFORE HE'D HEARD THAT TWIG SNAP. His night vision wasn't going to be worth much. Ehren and Reesa looked to be in the same state. Qalas ... possibly.

So only Amra was likely to have persevered her night vision, even though she, too, had been facing the fire.

A trick she had yet to teach Cavan in their travels.

Still, this was only the first night past the full moon, and this small section of woods had little canopy over the clearing. Cavan could see well enough to the tree line.

But not well enough to see the intruder.

"We have food to share," Ehren called out, using one hand to waft the smell of his roasting chickens and vegetables, though with the other he still picked up his goldenwood staff. "And a fire. There's no need for trouble."

Amra did nothing more than shift her sitting position, but she looked ready to fight. Her eyes kept moving though. As though even she could not yet spot who or what had snapped that twig.

Qalas had his hand on his weapon, and Cavan kept his hands near his belt, ready for sword or spell as he deemed necessary.

But something had sounded off about that snapping twig. If only Cavan could pick out what.

A war cry echoed into the night. Two dozen raiders ran into the camp, from all sides.

Ghostly raiders. Their skin, armor and weapons silvery and translucent. Their cries hollow.

Cavan and Amra drew their swords all the same, though Cavan did not take a ready pose.

More ghosts melted up through the ground. A dozen, men and women, kitted for war in full plate and shield, with longswords.

"Gah!" Qalas cried out, followed shortly by similar cries from Reesa and Ehren as the ghostly knights passed through them.

Cavan held his tongue through the experience. He'd had ghosts pass through him before, though it was not a sensation he relished.

The cold, wet sensation was famous and expected. What could never be planned on was the vivid flash of how that ghost had died.

And in the cases of these ghosts, their ends were bloody and quick.

The flash that Cavan experienced was like getting his throat slashed with a sword that hadn't been sharpened in far too long. It tore as much skin and muscle as it sliced, but the muscles behind the blow were more than adequate for the task.

The sensation faded just as the splash of pulsing blood began.

Cavan had been ready for it, but still he shivered. And he sheathed his sword. An enchanted metal like *licha* might be able to disrupt this ghostly reenactment, and that could have ... consequences.

He tried to content himself with studying the battle, that he might later learn the history of it. Perhaps even return, to help lay these spirits to rest.

The ghostly knights were sleepy. Slow. Perhaps exhausted from long days of marching or riding...

Riding. Cavan could see the ghosts of their horses off surrounding the clearing, being butchered by more ghostly raiders.

The hollow echo of steel meeting steel. Raiders dying. Knights dying.

Arrows flew into the fight, striking both sides interchangeably with unerring accuracy and chilling speed.

Elvish arrows. Even through their silvered forms, Cavan could see the spell-hardened bone heads, and the spell-aided fletchings.

Not many arrows. No more than half a dozen. But enough to swing the fight, as they struck down more knights than raiders.

Qalas hunched at his bedroll, halberd up and ready, but useless against the things that would not harm him anyway.

Reesa had a dagger in her hand, her face pale and drawn with fear, but she stayed steady.

Ehren had begun to pray, not that Cavan could imagine what good that would do. Zatafa was not a goddess of death, and she held no special means to lay these spirits to rest. Not in their current condition.

Only a psychopomp, a priest of the god of death, could do that.

Amra, of course, enjoyed the show more than Cavan thought was seemly. These people all died here, condemned for some reason to replay their deaths when the circumstances were right.

But Amra crouched, her sword in hand and fire in her eyes, as she seemed to be predicting each strike and each death to herself before they happened. As though she were studying this scene, not for its history, but for its tactics.

With her sword in hand.

That strange magic sword, that Cavan suspected to have been forged from the body of a demon...

"Amra," Cavan called quickly. "Sheathe your—"

He was too late.

Amra turned, following the battle.

A raider rushed out of the woods, at just the wrong angle. Where she could see the movement, but only just detected the possible threat as the raider's blade came down.

Battled tested reflexes did the rest.

Amra slipped backwards and cut for the throat of the raider.

Her strange magic sword cut right through his ghostly flesh. Sliced his head off in a fountain of silvery blood.

Her sword came away clean, Cavan noted through the shock of what he saw. Even the stuff of ghosts could not stick to that blade.

The flow of blood faded quickly, along with the rest of the interrupted battle scene.

The ground beneath them rumbled.

"That's not good, is it?" Amra asked.

"Killing ghosts," Qalas said. "How can that possibly be good? Amra, I can't believe you—"

"I didn't mean to," Amra said, frowning. Though Cavan thought he saw a pleased sparkle in her green-and-gold eyes that her sword could cut through even the substance of ghosts.

"There was intention behind the strike."

Words not spoken by Cavan, nor any of his friends. Words that echoed in a voice as deep as a dwarf's mine, and as hollow as a goblin's promise.

Wings unfolded in the blackness of the sky above them.

Cavan had only seen wings that large once before. In the Dragon Spikes, while attempting to scale the mighty peak known as the Dragon's Tooth, Cavan had seen more than his share of nests belonging to rocs, the giant birds that made their homes among the upper peaks, and hunted the nearby lands.

Among all the rocs he saw fly in and out of those nests, he had once caught a glimpse of the largest of them all. A roc so tremendous it could have carried off a castle in each of its claws.

The black wings unfolding in the air above Cavan now were big enough to have been carrying that roc.

Unfortunately, they were carrying something much worse.

Cavan had seen twenty summers since his birth.

He'd managed to live nineteen of them without ever meeting the divine face-to-face. Something he had not, until recently, regarded as an accomplishment.

Indeed, it was something he had managed to never think about at all.

And yet, only a few weeks ago, Cavan had passed through a gateway deep under a mountain that led to the Underworld of an ancient Dunaian god.

A god that recognized Cavan's line, confirming that he was indeed descended at least partially from that lost, powerful race of people.

Cavan and his friends had managed to escape that Underworld with their lives, but the price had been high. Power, the like of which Cavan might not see again in his lifetime.

He remembered that encounter in his dreams on more nights than he would admit.

On the nights he woke from those dreams in an icy sweat, he heard echoing once more that god's final words to him.

Farewell, Cavan Oltblood. We will *meet again.*

Cavan sincerely hoped that was not prophecy. So far as he was concerned, meeting gods should be left to their most devout followers. Like Ehren, with his Zatafa.

And yet, what floated in the air above him now could only be a messenger of Istanlos, the god of death.

Held up by black, batlike wings wider across than the small woods where Cavan and his friends had made their camp, was a creature large enough to need those wings.

It bore the shape of a human skeleton. Almost. Cavan could only see it from the torso up, and even what he saw was not quite human in design. Its elbows had spikes, and two ram's horns protruded from a skull in which all the teeth were fanged.

Also, this skeleton was not made of bone.

It looked as though it were made from rock and lava not yet spewed forth by a volcano. The whole of it was an ashen shade of black, but rivulets of bright reds and yellows ran all through the bones.

In its hands, the great winged skeleton held a flail that looked to have been made from the same dark metal as Amra's sword.

A resemblance that was likely the cause of the thoughtful sound he heard her utter then, as he, Amra, Ehren, Qalas, and Reesa all stared up at the great divine agent above them, only Reesa not on her feet.

Worse than the sight of the thing itself, or the implications of its presence, was the effect the messenger seemed to have on the world all about it.

Those pale evergreens that made up this small forest? They seemed washed out of color, as well as their sweet scent.

The fire in the center of the camp seemed to shed less light, and hardly any heat. Certainly not enough to roast the chickens and vegetables Ehren had arranged. Though their savory smells had faded as well to a mere suggestion of what they'd been only moments before.

These changes reminded Cavan all too clearly of the journey he, Ehren and Amra had made along the borderlands between worlds. As close as Cavan had ever wanted to come to the land of the dead. At least, while still breathing.

It was Amra who spoke first, answering the divine messenger's accusation.

"No true warrior can strike without intention," she said, and Cavan had to admit that even she sounded respectful at the moment. "But I swear that it was a strike made without deliberation. A reaction to the blow that I saw coming at my head. I could not have foreseen the results any more than I could have stopped my arm."

Cavan thought he heard Qalas muttering something in disbelief about arguing with gods.

"Do you contest the judgment of Istanlos?"

"Great Zirtax," Ehren said, hands apart and voice full of respect, "in Zatafa's name I ask that you forgive this one's hasty words."

Amra shot Ehren a pointed look, but the pristine priest kept talking.

"We do not understand what we disturbed this night, nor the nature of the crime committed, nor what judgment has been rendered by He Who Oversees the End of All."

"Istanlos holds no love for Zatafa," that empty voice said without the jaw of the skull moving in the least. *"But your request is fairly taken, priest. The tableau you witnessed tonight stood as the record of a great offense. An act anathema to Istanlos."*

Zirtax pointed an accusing finger.

"You five have disrupted the sequence, and yet not one of you is a psychopomp. You cannot lay these spirits to rest, so it is the judgment of Istanlos that you avenge the anathema, and see the remains to a psychopomp."

"Five of us?" Amra said. "I alone swung the sword that—"

"You have until the dark of the moon. Fail, and I will come for you."

And just like that, the divine messenger was gone from the night sky.

Color leapt back with almost blinding force. The ring of trees around the clearing, the sparkle of stars up in the heavens, and most of all the fire, so near and once again, so warm. Even Amra had to avert her eyes.

The savory smells of roasting chicken and vegetables, so welcome that Cavan's stomach wasn't alone in rumbling aloud.

"Don't," Amra said, turning a warning finger on Ehren. "Not a word."

Qalas stared back and forth between the short but deadly warrior and the taller priest.

Ehren raised his hands in surrender. His face absent its usual smile. And yet he spoke.

"I had only been wondering if any of us knew where to find a temple of Istanlos in this region. Assuming we complete the first part of our task, we will still need to find one of death's priests to lay these spirits to rest."

Amra narrowed her eyes suspiciously.

"Truly," Ehren said. "And lest you wonder, had I stood where you did, I might have swung my staff. And my reflexes are nothing to yours."

Amra nodded, still suspicious.

"Same here," Cavan said. "By the time I realized what your sword might do, I was too late to warn you. And even then, I could never have foreseen *that*."

"I could've," Qalas said, but when Amra whirled on him, he let his halberd fall and raised his hands. "I've heard of such things happening, down in the south. But I was only worried about *Cavan's* sword, because the tales told of *licha* blades cleaving ghosts."

Qalas frowned at Cavan. "I always thought those tales were just products of a bard's imagination."

Reesa looked from one to another, frowning in puzzlement. Likely worried that Amra might have actually turned her weapons on her friends.

Even Amra's temper wouldn't have gone *that* far.

Likely, the worst any of them would've gotten would've been a punch. Not that Cavan was eager to feel Amra's fist, if he didn't have to.

But this was not the time to explain these things to Reesa.

"I say we eat, and sleep," Cavan said, "and tomorrow we figure out just what happened here that Istanlos would consider anathema, and what we can do about it."

"Fair enough," Amra said, finally easing down to sit on her bedroll again, while Ehren finished preparing dinner.

"One thing's for sure," Qalas said, addressing Reesa. "Looks like you'll get your taste of adventure after all."

"He's right," Ehren said. "The task was given to the five of us. If any of us tried to shirk, Istanlos would not take it well."

Reesa's breaths were shallow, and Cavan could see fear in her wide eyes. But he had to admit, she held her chin up, determined, as though unwilling to shrink at the task before them.

An admirable trait. Cavan could only hope it would last.

4

Cavan awoke exactly when he intended, a full hour before dawn.

Amra was already up, and from the sweat on her brow and skin, looked to have finished her own morning workout already. She crouched, tending the fire, keeping it low but not quite out.

She seemed to be lost in her thoughts, staring into the flames. Just as well, Cavan wasn't ready for conversation yet.

He took his sword and stepped out of the clearing, into a place where the trees grew at least an arm's length apart, but not more than double that. A spot where the undergrowth was thin enough not to interfere.

Cavan drew his sword, and began his morning workout.

Not merely repeating the sequences of his training anymore. He still did that every so often, but these days he preferred a different approach.

He treated the trees around him as attacking foes. He danced among them, spinning one way or the other, parrying high now, low now, cutting out at the heights that best suited the enemies in his imagination. The undergrowth made his footing uneven, but to Cavan that only made the exercise more useful.

With his free hand, he pulled dirt from the mock spell pouch he kept beside his true spell pouch. Chanted half-spells that, if completed, would have blinded foes, or distracted them. In a few cases, would have done even more damage than Cavan could with his sword.

During his morning training, Cavan never completed any spells, out of respect for magic. No spell should be spoken in full, except to bring about its effects.

He continued until he'd lathered up a decent sweat. Only then did he pause to rest.

"Too regular," Amra said, quietly, from closer among the trees than Cavan expected. She did watch him work out sometimes, he knew that, but she always seemed to approach from a different distance and angle.

"The concept behind your training is sound," she continued, "but you need to vary the weapons and speed of the foes in your head. Right now, it's too easy for you to fall into patterns."

She frowned. "And you rely too heavily on the high parries. A man of your height will face more midline and low strikes."

"Thank you," Cavan said, stopping before her and giving her a slight bow, as though she were his formal instructor. Which got him the raised eyebrow it always did.

He been through her criticisms enough times that he could process her words, while still enjoying the good singing of his muscles and the light sheen of sweat matting his short brown hair.

"One more thing," she said, smacking his left shoulder. "Watch your guard when you go for your spells, and just before. Won't take more than one spell before your opponents realize they need to disable your left hand. And when you reach for the pouch, it will become a priority."

"I don't usually throw many in a fight."

"And if they know your reputation?" Amra fluttered her eyelashes that dangerous way of hers. "If it were me, I'd disable that arm before you had the chance to use it at all."

"Then it's a good thing the ruby" — Cavan patted the ruby in the pommel of his sword — "is tuned right to hold spells. My little emergency supply. And, of course, my spelled dagger."

"Wouldn't matter," Qalas said, approaching with halberd in hand. "Either of them. She'd kill you before you could get a spell off."

Amra nodded, matter of fact.

Cavan didn't bother to deny it. He just wandered back toward the camp while Qalas took his own turn loosening up before the day's adventures.

Ehren yet slept on his bedroll, near the sweet scent of the burning evergreen branches of the fire.

Oh, he would awaken before dawn, especially as he had healing to do. But Cavan felt inwardly pleased to have awakened before the smiling priest, for a change.

"I'm sorry," Reesa said, her voice not much above a whisper, from where she sat among the blankets of her nearby bedroll. Her shoulder-length, honey blond hair sleep-mussed in a way Cavan might have found appealing, were he not distracted by the sorrow in her tone and in her soft, gray eyes.

"Hush," Cavan said, just as softly, as he stepped lightly over to sit beside her, where he would not interfere with the comfort of her still-broken foot.

"It's my fault," she said. "None of this would have happened if not for me."

"Here now," Cavan tried, but Reesa had more to get out.

"You rushed out of town because of me. You left the road because of me."

"*We left the road,*" Cavan said, gently interrupting, "because that road was going west and our path lies north. Or at least it did. We often leave roads that go the wrong direction."

His attempt at levity fell on deaf ears.

"Nevertheless," she said, voice firm enough that Cavan let her finish. "You would have left Drien by the north road. You would not have come within leagues of this place. Amra would not have done what she did. And we would not have the task set us now."

"Finished?" Cavan asked.

That got him a suspicious look, but Reesa nodded.

"Search for first causes and you'll go mad. You and I are not where we sit now because of any one choice in either of our lives, but because of *every* choice we've made in *both* our lives."

Reesa drew her lips in and frowned, but it was a thoughtful frown, at least.

"You wanted to be an adventurer?" Cavan asked. "Well, it's a messy life, full of mistakes and questionable choices. And the truth is, often we can only tell the mistakes in retrospect."

"Oh, come on…" Reesa started, but Cavan kept talking.

"You listed ways we *might* have avoided this task. However, through this task we stand to right a wrong, and lay restless spirits to rest. That sounds worthwhile to me, so who's to say our being here is a 'mistake?'"

"But the risk…"

"Life is risk," Cavan said with a lopsided smile. "Only death is certain."

"So," Reesa said softly. So softly Cavan could almost not hear her words over the distant scuffling of Qalas' workout and the gentle crackling of the fire. "You aren't sorry you met me?"

Cavan looked deep into those soft, gray eyes.

"Not in any way."

And truth be told, this might have been the best opening Cavan could have hoped for to discuss the subject that lay between them. Their night together, and what it might or might not mean, going forward.

But that moment, of course, was when Ehren spoke.

"Careful, Cavan," the priest said through his trademark smile as he sat up and began to tie back his long, sun-blond hair. "You're beginning to show signs of wisdom."

"I'll try not to make a habit of it," Cavan said, returning the smile, though he didn't quite feel it inside.

"Then at least move aside so I can see what a hurried ride, a divine threat, and a rough night's sleep have done to my patient."

Cavan withdrew then, while Ehren checked Reesa's wounds.

Amra waved him over to where she was preparing the horses for their day's ride, while Qalas continued limbering up.

A welcome enough break. There would be time for personal concerns later.

As PREDAWN LIGHTENED THE CERULEAN SKY ABOVE THE GIANT TREES OF the Wailing Woods far to the east, Cavan stood with Amra and Qalas to one side of the fire, while on the other side Ehren stood beside Reesa, who reclined on her bedroll.

Qalas had his head bowed respectfully. Cavan and Amra had their eyes on Ehren, ready to watch once more what Cavan considered the greatest wonder the smiling priest could perform.

Reesa lay with Cavan's red tunic open to show the bruises on her ribs, but her chest otherwise covered, and the boot, poultices and bandages that had protected her broken foot stripped down to flesh. She still wore the leather leggings she'd worn for her duel, but then, she might not see a change of clothes for quite some time.

Cavan supposed it was a good thing he'd started carrying a second tunic, after the first time he lost one.

Ehren faced the east. He held his staff high. He began to chant in Penthix, in praise of Zatafa (the only word Cavan understood of the prayers).

The first shaft of dawn crested the horizon. It struck Ehren and enveloped him in a golden glow. His hair now all the colors of sunlight, and his clear blue eyes an island of peace.

He looked natural, that way. As though he should have always had such a halo surrounding him. As though the way he moved through his day-to-day life were a mere disguise, to not disturb the masses.

While Ehren chanted, he lowered the tip of his staff and touched Reesa's worst injury: her foot.

She moaned, and Cavan knew well the feeling of the immense healing relief that Ehren spread through this prayer. A blissful kind of warmth that spread throughout the body, knitting nearly any wounds and ills a person might suffer.

By the time Ehren lifted away the tip of his staff, she all but glowed with health, and looked as fresh and clean as though she and her clothes had both just been laundered. Her hair even looked freshly brushed out.

Cavan had expected the healing to end with Reesa, but Ehren did not stop there.

He turned to each of Cavan, Amra and Qalas and touched them with the staff as well.

Relief. Such relief that Cavan knew that even his memory would fall short of it, once the true bliss of the moment passed.

Cavan had not been wounded as Reesa had, that was true. But the touch of Zatafa's light through that prayer eased even Cavan's worries and concerns about Reesa, and what he and she might or might not mean to one another.

There would be time for those questions. They would keep until that time came.

And the blessing did more than that.

Little aches from the road. Little strains to the muscles. All the tiny discomforts that Cavan knew well from travels and sleepless nights faded, replaced only by a sense of vitality and well-being.

Even Amra was smiling and content when Ehren stepped to the edge of the clearing to bestow the blessing on their horses.

Only when he finished there did the halo fade from around Ehren. He raised his head and hands to the dawn once more, cried out in praise of Zatafa, and turned to face Cavan and the others.

"The horses," Reesa said as she stood and stretched, visibly enjoying her lack of pain. She buttoned up the red tunic as she continued, "Why weren't they terrified by the apparitions last night? I sure was."

"The glory of Zatafa, of course." Ehren's smile broadened. "I bless them every night before we dine. Primarily it is a safeguard against..." — Ehren glanced at Cavan and back at Reesa — "but it seems that the blessing *also* soothes them against the presence of apparitions that cannot harm them."

"It was *one time*," Cavan said, but Ehren laughed, and Amra and Qalas joined him.

Even Reesa smiled, but it was a hesitant kind of smile. As though she wanted to join in the wholehearted laughter, but wasn't sure she should. So she focused on lacing up her knee-high boots.

Truth was, Cavan couldn't muster that much irritation. He felt too good at the moment. And besides, his experiments were not always ... as effective as he would have liked.

And it was true that his failures could spook horses and other animals. Sometimes, at least.

The blessing left everyone in high spirits as they broke their fast on good, sharp cheese, toasted sausages, and fine, dark Oltoss rye, as well as skins of spring water.

Cavan and his friends, by mutual agreement, never began serious discussions until after they had eaten in the morning. Well, unless matters pressed enough that they could not wait.

This left an opening for Reesa to ask a question Cavan had long since stopped worrying about.

"Those chickens last night," she said to Ehren, holding a hot, half-eaten apple sausage speared on a stick. "As well as all this."

"Yes?" Ehren said with an even wider smile than usual, mirth dancing in his eyes.

"You never went to the packs on the horses. All of this came out of —" she pointed at Ehren's backpack with her sausage — "that?"

"I sometimes think," Amra said thoughtfully, "that he could produce a fully crewed warship from that backpack, if he needed one."

"How would he get it in, in the first place?" Qalas asked.

"A plank at a time," Amra said, smiling now and warming to the topic, "along with shipwrights, sailmakers, and the rest of whatever the ship needed."

"That's assuming," Cavan joined in — he couldn't help himself — "that he needs to put something in to pull it out. What if—"

"If I may," Ehren said, and Amra bowed her head in smiling deference to him. At least, on this topic, and for the time being.

Cavan and Qalas nodded to him, encouragingly.

"Thank you," Ehren said, then turned to Reesa. "In truth, I suspect this backpack holds more secrets than even I know, and I've been its custodian these past fifteen summers."

"Custodian?" Reesa asked, around a mouthful of sausage.

"That is how I choose to see my role," he answered with a shrug. "I was but a boy, studying at the temple then. During morning prayers one day, a wounded man burst in."

Ehren frowned at the memory. "His heritage, impossible to place. I would have sworn he had the thick teeth and shoulders of a man with orc blood, but the fine, almost pointed ears and tree bark brown shade to his skin as though he had forest elf blood. And yet the better part of his features seemed human."

"What was he fleeing?"

"We never got to find out. Whatever it was, it never reached us. Perhaps it could not approach a place sacred to Zatafa." Ehren shrugged. "I reached the dying man first. He reeked of blood and sweat, offal and hard travel. I gave him water. There was little else to do, save prepare him for his journey to the afterlife. His entrails hung behind him, and some of them were missing. He didn't even have much blood left to bleed."

"What happened?"

"I was the first to reach him, but others were only a step behind. They began assessments of what, honestly, we already knew but needed to verify, and then to do what our prayers could do to ease his suffering before he passed beyond."

Ehren drew a long, slow breath. The air was still enough that Cavan could hear each pop of the fire, and the distant cry of a wrest bird.

"He did not try to save his own life. Most men, they would have clutched their entrails. Tried to stuff them back inside, as if by primal need. The recognition that what was outside needed to be inside."

Ehren slowly shook his head. His voice grew quieter. As somber as Cavan ever heard him.

"Instead, he clutched this backpack instead of bits of himself." Ehren shook his head again, slowly. "I do not know if I could have done the same."

Ehren blinked as though coming out of a trance.

"Either way, as his last act in this world, he thrust this backpack past two other, more advanced novitiates and into my arms. His lips moved with words, but I could not hear them, and I did not recognize the pattern his lips formed."

"I have been its custodian ever since. And though I sincerely doubt that its interior could provide the air needed for living beings" — Ehren raised a droll eyebrow at Amra — "anything else I can fit inside it, seems to await my need."

"So you *do* have to put things in, before you can take them out," Qalas said. "I'd started to wonder."

"Perhaps," Ehren said, mirth in his eyes again and his natural smile back in place. "Or perhaps its custodian must keep certain secrets to himself."

"In either case," Cavan said through a deep breath, "we've finished eating. And now we have more weighty matters before us."

Comparing details about what Cavan and his friends had noticed during the ghostly battle did not take long. It was the sort of thing that three of them had done many times before — gone over something they'd witnessed, to make sure they each had all information available for their assessments.

Qalas had only been through it once or twice, for he had not been with them all that long, but he had fallen quickly into the efficient, swift distribution of information.

Each person made statements about what he or she observed, first the simple facts, then conclusions that could be drawn with a high degree of certainty. Lower certainty speculations were left for later, and all questions were confined to details and clarifications.

Reesa, of course, had probably never seen anything like this before. But then, Cavan suspected that she had never seen anything like a ghostly battle scene before either. So she would most certainly have been excused, had she failed to contribute anything to the general knowledge base.

Amra began things, of course. She had noted the arms and armor of the raiders, their numbers — a dozen knights attacked by twice that many raiders — as well as that those raiders struck on foot, yet slaughtered horses.

This meant that their own horses were hobbled in the distance, likely toward the outside edge of the small woods, in the direction they'd ridden from.

These details also meant that the raiders knew exactly where to find their foes, what they needed to do once they found them, and that there was no risk of returning with booty they could not carry.

In other words, this was no simple banditry. Even the most incompetent bandits would keep horses rather than butcher them.

This assault was intended as a massacre.

Ehren did not know much of tactics or weapons, but he noted that the knights had seemed to keep no watch. Every one of the ghostly knights had arisen as though from sleep. So they clearly felt they were in safe territory. He also raised the question — in case anyone had observed a potential answer — of why they were traveling together.

Amra, however, pointed out that they might have had scouts or watchers who were killed in silence, before the battle proper had begun.

Reesa suggested they might have been part of a larger force.

Amra pointed out, however, that a battle like the one they witnessed would have been heard for some distance. Drawn aid for the knights, if they'd had a larger force nearby.

No slouch with a bow himself, Qalas had more to say about the archery. The raiders had brought only the one archer, which he,

Cavan, and Amra all agreed was strange. The knights all wore armor. Why would the raiders not soften up their foes before the slaughter?

And yet, only one archer fired arrows into the melee. An archer who waited until the battle was well underway, then struck with the accuracy — and the fletchings — of a forest elf. Further, the archer seemed to show no concern over whether his or her arrows struck knights or raiders.

Or, to be more precise, that archer targeted both sides.

Amra then postulated that both sides needed to die during the fight.

Discussing that took some time, because it seemed so unusual from a tactical perspective, but Cavan tied it all together with an observation of his own.

Cavan pointed out that if both sides died by violence, while battling each other, their spirits would be filled with the fire of combat. That passion, that bloodlust, would cling to their spirits, as well as seep into the very bones of the combatants when their bodies died.

Cavan's theory: necromancy.

The necromancer would have had to act quickly, to achieve the maximum benefit from the slaughter. The passions of the dying were known to fade rapidly from their bodies, though Cavan believed the effect on the spirit lasted longer.

But then, Cavan's knowledge of necromancy was cursory and theoretical.

Still, the concept was troubling enough that he had to pursue his theory to its end.

Cavan's theory continued that it was likely that the raiders, and the archer, were both sent by the same necromancer to slaughter the knights. The raiders likely didn't know the archer existed until the arrows started flying. The archer made sure no one left alive, and reported back when the battle finished.

The necromancer could then have come to the woods and raised a number of ... high quality servants.

Cavan hadn't been able to call them "good" servants.

In fact, Cavan considered it the most likely possibility that the necromancer had ridden out with the archer as his or her personal guard, in order to be on hand as soon as the slaughter was complete.

Ehren confirmed that wanton slaughter for necromancy was just the sort of thing that Istanlos would regard as a great offense. All the more so if the knights had been in the service of the necromancer in the first place.

That was a thought none of them enjoyed, but none could dispute was a possibility.

Amra pointed out that there may have been a more mundane answer. It might have been a noble hiring raiders to be rid of a rival and that rival's supporters. The raiders would have been killed to remove witnesses.

If so, there was a simple way to determine which theory was more likely correct.

They spread out and searched the area.

Alas, it did not take long to determine that no graves or cairns stood nearby. And digging shallowly into the dirt showed no signs that bones had simply been left behind, either, to say nothing of any armor and weapons.

No, it seemed to be likely that Cavan was right. And that the necromancer might even have raised the horses to serve in death, as they had in life.

And this was why Ehren, Amra, Qalas and Reesa all then stood to one side of the clearing, while Cavan alone stood in the center.

The fire had been extinguished and its remains scattered. The bedrolls all gathered and put back in the saddle bags of their horses.

The clearing was as smooth as they could make it, given their attempts to discover any lingering remains.

Cavan did not relish what he had to do. Detecting active magic and strong enchantments, that sort of work was easy. If they were strong enough, he did not even need a spell to enhance his perceptions.

Even lingering spells could draw his attention, if they were the right type of spells.

But this...

Cavan had no way of knowing how much time had passed since the necromancer had raised all these knights, raiders, and steeds. Assuming Cavan had been right in the first place. Assuming that this was what happened.

It might have been...

No.

This was not the time for might-have-beens.

Cavan believed he was right. Ehren seemed to agree that it would be sufficient offense against Istanlos to cause that scene to be repeated. And to get them this quest.

Besides, if Cavan was wrong, he would recover from the blinding headache.

Cavan stood alone in the center of the dirt clearing. Overhead the sky was clear, and pale blue. The sun still hours from its apex. He stood ringed by pale evergreens whose breed and nature he did not know.

Ordinarily, that would have been fine. But for what Cavan was doing now, what he did not know could prove dangerous.

So the first thing he did was note the evergreens, each of the closest about a half-dozen strides away. Their dark needles smelled sweet, slightly sticky. Their bark, so much more like beech in color than even the pines Cavan had seen around Drien.

Cavan drew slow, deep breaths of late summer air. Cool, this far north, but not yet cold. Hints of rain on the air, coming west from the Wailing Woods. But rain that would not be here until at least the morrow.

Cavan separated out the feel of that breeze on his skin, the scent of rain it carried. Narrowed his focus onto the trees.

Twice before, Cavan had met trees that could uproot themselves and walk. Could lash out with their limbs, and even creak and groan in patterns that formed a language of a kind.

Cavan had learned to feel the nature of such trees, to ensure that he never unknowingly harmed one.

These evergreens around Cavan now, they were not walking trees. Though Cavan might not know their breed, he could tell now with certainty that they were trees like most others. None even played host to dryads, or other active forest spirits. Or at least, none close enough to merit Cavan's attention at the moment.

One layer of potential interference removed.

The next would have been Cavan's friends, but they had been good enough to remove themselves out of the clearing into the woods. Not by far, it was true, but far enough that their presence would not matter much.

This clearing might not have formed a perfect circle, but it was not far off. It was close enough that, if Cavan was right, a necromancer could confine his magics within it.

Now that Cavan was confident that nothing along the ring of the clearing could distract him, he was ready to proceed with his working.

The limitations of Cavan's aborted training would make his task only more difficult. Had he been fully trained, he might have known conjugations and declensions of the verb *Neel*, which governed most forms of magical detection, that would have stretched further into the past. Or any of the right place nouns to target his efforts. Perhaps even the nouns for the right kind of...

But Cavan did not know these things, and he thrust from his attention concerns about knowledge he did not possess.

Instead, he focused on what he *could* do, and how he believed he could determine what magics, if any, had been done here.

Cavan began with the simplest approach. All part of tuning himself to understand what was now, so he could better determine what was *then*.

"*Neela asa,*" he whispered, and gave himself time to adjust to the enhancement of his wizard sight.

Those pale evergreens all now glowed flickering green with the auras of their lives. The reds and yellows of his friends, easily spotted, then ignored. The sky above, paled from blues to faint shades of gray.

And here within the clearing itself, the ground...

The dirt here should, if anything, have become a darker brown. Full of the potential of life, or perhaps flickering here and there with the auras of other things worth finding, if they happened to be near enough to the surface.

In fact, if there were bodies or other remains here within the clearing, especially remains of those who had died by violence, Cavan would have spotted violet tinges or flashes to mark them.

But the dirt here had a faint aura of a deep vermilion.

That was a sign of magical interference here. Some great working, if not recent.

Had Cavan been a better wizard, he might have been able to puzzle through characteristics about that working from the aura that remained. But it was too old for him. Too faint. All the clues that a more powerful wizard might have gleaned from merely examining the aura were clues that lay beyond his skill.

But Cavan was definitely on the right track. And he knew a way to learn what he needed to know.

The key then, was to hook into that aura, and trace it back to its roots.

Cavan gave himself to the working then. He might not have been fully trained as a wizard, but he had continued his training on his own after he was sent away by Master Powys. Cavan had kept up all the exercises, and continued to push and learn as much as he could, whenever he had the opportunity.

What was more, Cavan had combined his lessons in wizardry with those things he had learned in his training to become a warrior.

No matter what Amra would have said, the two approaches had interesting parallels.

One such parallel was that, when the time came to act, the time to think had passed.

So Cavan trusted to his limited training and broader experience. He chanted, focusing on his goal rather than the words he chose.

Gestured when his hands knew to gesture. And pulled the right bits of herbs and other components whenever the spell he was developing called for them.

In this way, Cavan dug a path into that vermilion aura, and traced it back through time itself. Gripped and clung and climbed through the past, while the aura seemed to fight him, shifting and twisting as though to throw off his mind and leave Cavan's sense of self somewhere in the past, perhaps even with no way back to his body.

But of tenacity Cavan had a surfeit. He clung and chanted and pushed his way deeper through that aura. Compelling, then demanding that it reveal the secrets of its origin.

At first, this showed him nothing but the aura itself, an all-encompassing color that carried with it a kind of distant cold.

But Cavan fought and struggled with that aura, as though he were catching a fish with his bare hands, and it represented the first food he'd even *seen* in over a week.

Sometimes, in any struggle, the held and the holder twist the same way at the same time. In that moment, it is as though the holder needs no effort at all.

Cavan achieved such a moment and used it to thrust as far as he could, as fast as he could, into the depths of that vermilion aura.

A trap lay waiting.

Just like that, the vermilion was gone.

Darkness. Confinement on all sides. Cavan, in a coffin. The coffin underground. Chilling to the bone. The smell of decay, grave mold and ancient dust.

Not just a coffin. Chains. Just as ancient. Iron colder than death itself. Fixed to his wrists and arms, ankles and legs.

Cavan's armor, gone. His sword, his pouch of spells, even his friends — all gone. Cavan alone. Confined. Facing the end of all.

What heat Cavan possessed leached out of him through those chains. Slowly. Like bleeding to death by drops.

No.

There had to be a way through this. Out of it. He was not in a coffin. He was not chained. Cavan knew these things. His body stood in a dirt clearing while his mind dug into the details of a spell...

And yet that chill was there, leaching away his strength. His sense of self. His limbs, unmoving. No way to escape.

No! This simply could not be.

Cavan summoned to his mind the image of that vermilion aura. The feel of it, its distant chill a different quality than the very present chill all about him.

The vermilion aura was a truth. Its distant cold was a truth. The clearing was a truth. This casket, these ancient iron chains, these things were lies.

All of the bindings on Cavan, they were lies.

He was caught in a lie.

Truth. The answer was truth. He needed truth stronger than the lies that held him.

Cavan pressed against those lies with the truth of the spell he sought — its aura, its chill — but it was too new, too unknown. The source of more questions than answers.

This truth was not strong enough to save him.

Cavan tried the truth of his task. A quest from no lesser being than the god of death itself. To solve the riddle of the slaughter. Trace its cause. Avenge the wrong. Set the restless spirits free.

But death was known well in this place where Cavan was trapped. Death was the endgame here, not the pathway out. He could plead his failure to Istanlos all too soon...

No!

This trap was an *illusion*. No matter how tightly it held him, it was a *lie*. Cavan merely needed a stronger truth to burn his way past it. Not a simple truth like love for his friends or his sense of responsibility or his own thirst to prove himself as both a wizard and a warrior.

The trap was too strong for those things. Ready for them. Those thoughts only bound the chains tighter. Fed Cavan's efforts right back with a sense of doom, of inevitable failure. Cavan's warmth bled away faster still.

A place deep within Cavan began to ache with deep, icy cold. Freezing him outward from the core of his being.

Cavan needed a deeper truth. Something powerful enough that he had trouble confronting it, even to himself.

Cavan's only way through this would be to face something he did not want to face. A truth against which, remaining here to die might feel welcoming.

A truth that, even with Cavan in dire need, he did not enjoy bringing at last into his thoughts.

His mother.

The woman who abandoned him. The woman who would not admit to having bore him. As a child, Cavan had pestered Kent often for details about his mother. Anything his foster father would or could tell him.

Kent had refused all inquiries, saying only that Cavan's mother had not chosen to surrender him. That she loved him, and one day, she would come to see him when she could.

But that day had never come.

Cavan had grown into a man. Traveled, adventured, made a name for himself, until even his father had admitted being proud of his bastard. Had claimed that Cavan was more like him than any of his trueborn children.

Even King Draven had made time to see the child who had been such a political burden that, until that incident at the Ice Dagger, even publicly speaking Cavan's name would have carried dire consequences.

And still, Cavan had not yet seen even the least sign of his mother. Not so much as the slightest indication that she lived or had died, let alone that she might wish some role in Cavan's life. To say nothing of any desire to see what had become of her ... indiscretion with the king.

King Draven had denied Cavan because the queen's family was too powerful to risk insulting. As a child, that had been difficult for Cavan, but as he'd grown and traveled, he had come to understand it.

He did not like it, and he had held it against the king for a long time. But he had come to understand it. He had even come to forgive Draven, to an extent at least.

But if Cavan's mother had any such excuse, why had Cavan never heard it? Why were there no tales of her husband, or the political difficulties Cavan's existence put her to? Or even tales of her fleeing the shame of Cavan's birth, to take up some sort of ascetic life somewhere?

Even in Cavan's childhood, during the worst days of the political consequences of his existence, he remembered a handful of secret visits to secluded parts of the royal castle, for a few minutes of time with the man whose seed had given Cavan life.

And yet where, in all of Cavan's life was his mother?

Nowhere. Because she did not care. She did not merely give Cavan birth. She expelled him from her body, from her life, and from her thoughts.

And the truth that Cavan never faced all these years was a simple one.

He hated his mother.

It was not merely that she meant nothing to him, as he often tried to pretend. No. He hated her for abandoning him. For never sending so much as an inquiry about Cavan's health that Kent could have pointed to, to show Cavan that she even cared whether he lived or died.

Cavan *hated* his mother.

A foul, bitter truth. A painful truth. But a truth that carried power. Power enough to burst through the illusion and carry Cavan all the way to his destination at the heart of that vermilion aura.

THE CLEARING, NOW TINGED WITH ONLY HINTS OF THE VERMILION THAT Cavan's mind had traveled through. Even the mental projection of his own body, beneath him where Cavan stood, apparently still in the center of the clearing. Even he was tinged with vermilion, like the stars in the dark sky above him.

Dark sky. Not merely nighttime, then, here when the spell was cast. The dark of the moon.

It was said in Naresh, off to the west, that during nights of the dark moon, all the foul things of the world roamed freely to work their will. Angry spirits, wandering demons, murderous faeries.

An auspicious time for the darkest sorts of necromancy.

And all about Cavan, the stage was set for just such a working. The remains of a bloody slaughter.

All those knights, dead. All those raiders, dead. Even the horses, all dead.

Only one living thing stood within the clearing now.

The necromancer. Striding calmly into the center of the clearing, without regard for whether he stepped on dirt, blood, or bodies in those low boots that looked to have been fashioned from elk hide.

He didn't look the type. Or at least, he showed none of the outward signs of necromancy favored by bards in their tales. His eyes were neither glowing red nor dead black, but hazel, and the pupils were normal, not shaped like skulls.

The necromancer stood about middling height, perhaps a head shorter than Cavan. The top of the man's skull was tonsured, and what hair surrounded the tonsure was white and fluffy. Almost downy.

His skin had a ruddy hue to it, as though the age that had given the necromancer his many wrinkles had still left him glowing with life.

Or perhaps he kept that glow by stealing life from others.

No. That was speculation. Cavan was here to observe.

So Cavan noted the necromancer's height, and that his build kept to the thin edge of life. His robes were black, with traceries of dark blues and purples, in symbols that Cavan knew had arcane significance, even if they were symbols he did not, himself, recognize.

Whatever else he was, though, the necromancer was clearly powerful. He had an aura of power as strong as anything Cavan had seen since his encounter with that amazing orc shaman, Iresk the Hawkspeaker.

Alas, though, Cavan could not tell as much about that aura, here within a projection of the remnants of a spell, as he could have were he standing so close to the necromancer in person.

The necromancer carried no staff. That surprised Cavan. Most wizards past a certain age carried staves, if only because they had so many uses in spellwork. Apart, of course, from helping to cover any difficulties an aged wizard might have in getting around.

The necromancer had no such difficulties. He looked almost spry as he moved about, chanting keywords here, dribbling bits of grave dirt, crumbled mold, and ground bone there. Setting the circle not by drawing a circle, but by marking the key points with iron nails, to form a forbidden seven-sided star.

And that, as much as anything else, suggested that this was a necromancer. The seven-sided star had only one true use: binding the will of another.

Most often, from what Cavan had been taught by Master Powys, wizards with more daring than sense would use that star in their attempts to bind demons.

However, those of a certain bent who delved deeper into the mysteries of the seven-sided star would use the shape to bind the dead.

And that was what Cavan was watching right now.

The necromancer pulled a wand from up his sleeve. It looked to have been carved from a human thigh bone, yellowed with age, and so powerful that even without trying, Cavan could feel its aura.

The necromancer worked his fell magics then. He chanted and moved about, touching each fallen body with the tip of his wand, then anointing it with blood from different corpse — blood that Cavan noted was still fresh, which meant the necromancer had indeed been waiting nearby — by touching that blood to his own lips first, then kissing the corpse on the forehead.

And all the while, the necromancer continued his steady line of chanting. Words that slipped away from Cavan's ears as soon as he heard them. He could not so much as recognize a single verb of the spells, much less any of the nouns.

No, even watching the necromancer at work, Cavan had no idea of exactly how the man did what he did.

But somehow, even the part of Cavan that wanted to learn all of magic that he could was just fine missing out on this lesson.

Once the necromancer had bestowed his fell kiss on all of the dead bodies — including the horses — he returned to the center of the clearing.

There he took his wand and stabbed it at the night sky while crying out a single word. At least, Cavan was pretty sure the necromancer spoke only one word in time with that thrust. He had trouble being certain, because that word slammed into him with power.

Power that whisked through him, then came sweeping back, carrying with it a faint echo of the compulsion that made every single corpse, all around Cavan's awareness, rise and serve that necromancer.

Fortunately for Cavan, the compulsion carried no weight. Did not compel him to join them.

Still, even that hint of the power these poor souls had been subjected to only fired Cavan's anger at the abomination he was witnessing.

Cavan made himself turn to see every face, man, woman and horse. Make sure he knew exactly how many souls had been ensnared by this evil man's spells.

Cavan would see to it that every one of these souls were released, to move on to whatever reward or punishment awaited it in the afterlife.

And Cavan would see to it that this necromancer never had a chance to perform a rite like this again. Not if he could help it.

Cavan itched to return to his friends. To tell them what he saw. To feel their indignation match his own, so that together they could see about righting this wrong.

But no, Cavan forced himself to remain. Forced himself to witness all he could before he left.

And it was a good thing he did.

For Cavan watched the dead not only rise to serve that necromancer, but rise and move with the same grace and ease they had carried in life. Even though their eyes and faces showed none of the vibrancy of life.

What Cavan witnessed proved the truth of what he had only suspected as he observed the ritual. These were not merely shambling corpses, but a higher form of undead. The necromancer had not merely animated their flesh and bones, but bound the spirits to their fallen bodies.

Cavan did not know the word for what these poor souls had become. But he did know that would be even more difficult to face, if they formed the army that stood between Cavan and that necromancer.

Cavan watched as the necromancer led his new soldiers away from the clearing, toward the northeast.

That had to be the direction they needed to go then.

It might be the direction of the necromancer's abode, or it might be the enemy against which the necromancer wished to strike. But either way, something to the northeast would hold the clues Cavan and his friends would need to begin their quest.

He watched until the last of them passed from the clearing.

Then his spell was broken. And Cavan's real work could begin.

5

———

THE THREE ORCS PASSED BY, NEVER SUSPECTING HOW CLOSE THEY CAME to death.

Vastig lay among the tall, golden grasses of the hilltop. Concealed among nature as only a forest elf can be. Hardly worth thinking of as magic, though Vastig knew that the other races considered it so.

Vastig lay there, watching, as the three passed him by. He noted their arms: each carried a double-headed axe, but no bows. Slings, tied to their axe handles. The carried no bags nor pouches though, which meant if they wanted to use those slings, they'd have to scramble for rocks. Inefficient.

They wore togas made from the thick hide of some beast that never set foot in a forest, or Vastig would have known it. The hides looked thick enough to provide some semblance of armor.

Vastig made his mental notes as the orc scouts passed by. Never once did he so much as twitch. Stillness was a hunter's stock and trade, and a forest elf hunter had to be the best of the best.

Vastig was better still. And he knew it.

Most would have kept their swords sheathed, to avoid even accidental exposure of a reflection to a passing eye.

Vastig preferred to keep his weapons ready. And he knew the

perfect angle to lay his thin, twin blades along his thighs. Mere steel these days, instead of proper shaped and formed *zil* hardwood, but he had to work with what was available to him now.

The bow strapped to his back was an even more embarrassing example. Yes, it was double curved, and the finest gold could buy. Still it was inferior to the brilliance of a simple longbow made from *zil*.

But then, since his banishment, Vastig could at least pursue his interests in peace.

Vastig sniffed as the orcs passed, scenting not only the warm, midday dirt beneath him, nor the high wild grass his own people called *lisath*.

More important to smell those orcs.

They smelled like blood, of course. They always did. They cooked with it, blended it with their drinks. They smelled like rank sweat, and dirt as well, but that was their nature. That could not be helped.

More important to note the degree of sweat in their odor, and the quantity of dirt. From these things, Vastig knew that these three scouts had been on patrol for no more than half the time Vastig had been positioned here, and he had positioned himself just before the sunrise.

That meant that these three orcs were indeed the ones he'd seen in the distance, beginning their patrol. The timing matched.

Vastig now knew with certainty the rhythm of the patrols kept by the Red Blade tribe. He could give the scouts perhaps the time of a hawk's circle up above to return and report.

And then Vastig would rise from his hiding place. Slip in past their picket lines. Find some important orc. A splinter, perhaps. A favored cook. Someone important to the chief.

A child if the chief had children. A child would be best.

Oh, if only Vastig could slip away with an orc babe today. He would not feast as well as he would on an adult, but the flesh would be tender. A pleasant change from the general stringy texture of orc flesh.

Vastig's mouth was watering already.

He prepared to make his move.

And this was when he was interrupted.

"Vastig! The master commands!"

"Quiet, fool," Vastig said, rolling to his feet and trotting down the hillside away from the orc encampment. He did not know yet which of his master's servants had come to deliver orders, but whichever it was could damn well follow him to deliver them, rather than risk Vastig's discovery.

After days setting up what Vastig liked to call his next larder, it would be a shame for him to be spotted now.

At the foot of the hillside, Vastig held up a hand to stay the servant's report. First, he would sheathe his swords and clap the dust and loose grass from his clothes. The last proper forest elf clothes he might ever own.

They'd been beaten and shaped from tree bark, like most proper forest elf clothing. Vastig's were deep shades of brown and burnt orange that went well with his dark, gray-brown skin, and short, nut-brown hair.

Finally, he turned to see which servant the master had sent. That little bit of information would tell Vastig his own current standing in the eyes of the necromancer.

A spirit. The sort likely not visible to the naked eye of the lesser races, but easily spotted by an elf. This spirit looked to be orcish, which Vastig took as an insult, but it was old at least. Vastig could tell by the shade of it.

Newer spirits looked a cloying shade of white to his eyes, while as they aged they seemed to gain first a sort of translucence, followed by a yellowing. As though they were made from aged vellum, rather than the proper stuff of spirits.

This orcish spirit in front of Vastig now, it was more yellowed than white. So the necromancer was irritated with him for some reason, but still respectful.

Of course, that could also have been a show of superiority from the necromancer. A way to ensure Vastig felt the need to put forth his very best effort, to evade his master's displeasure.

Only one way to find out.

"Very well," Vastig said, giving the messenger the expected bow, if perfunctory. "You have my attention. What word from our master?"

"The master's words..."

And then the voice of the spirit changed from its normal bass, orcish tones, to the high, clear, human voice of the necromancer.

"Some fool has disturbed my trap in the clearing at the Forest of Risen Knights, but managed to escape. You are to investigate this disturbance. If it looks to cause me trouble, kill the interloper and bring me his heart and skull. Dispose of the rest as you would."

"And if it—"

"If the interloper flees, he is either too weak to be worth my time, or too craven for his spirit to be useful. In either case, you may deal with him in whatever manner you choose, so long as you silence him."

Vastig gave his master, through his master's representative, the sort of proper bow he would expect.

"I swear it shall be done, master."

"I know you will not fail me."

The spirit sailed off into the air then, without another word. But then, no more words were necessary. Failure would mean a change in the manner of Vastig's service. He would be drained of his lifeforce, and then forced to serve beyond death.

Of course, if Vastig failed a task such as this one, then as far as he was concerned he deserved such a fate.

In the meantime, he hoped the interloper fled. That would be worth abandoning the work he'd done to prepare for the Red Blade tribe.

Yes, if the interloper fled, then Vastig's real fun would begin.

6

———

When Cavan found himself leaving the vermilion world of that necromantic spell's history, at the end of his own investigatory working, he'd been more than ready to leap astride Dzint and set course at a gallop, yelling the details of what he'd learned to his friends as they rode off.

But as so often seemed to happen in Cavan's life, his intentions did not quite live up to his expectations.

Cavan's consciousness returned to his body, and slammed right into the reality of his situation.

First and foremost, the blinding headache given him by his working. The truth was that Cavan was insufficiently trained for the spell he'd performed. And though Cavan liked to pretend that all that stood between himself as he was and himself as a fully qualified wizard was time in a library with the right reading material, the fact was that he needed more than information to become a proper wizard.

A proper wizard underwent long series of exercises to prepare their minds for the lesser versions of what Cavan had just done. Cavan had experienced only the least of these exercises before Master Powys had sent him away, advising him to never again attempt even the things he had been training to do, to say nothing of anything beyond his meager training.

And so, the price that Cavan paid for attempting what he was unready to attempt was fiery pain throughout his skull, hazing the world in red so thick that Cavan could not tell which of his friends were running towards him as he fell to the dirt in the clearing.

He could not parse the sounds he heard then as words, let alone questions. He could not even tell Ehren's baritone from Reesa's high, sweet voice.

All Cavan could do was experience that horrible, all-consuming pain in his skull, until it would abate enough for him to begin applying what techniques he knew to rid himself of the rest.

There was little even an amazing healer such as Ehren could do for Cavan, as he lay there, writhing in pain. There were no true wounds to treat. Cavan was only dealing with spell fire: the aftereffects of channeling too much of the kinds of energies his mind was unprepared for.

But even as the eternity of blinding pain seemed to begin to abate — or perhaps Cavan had begun to acclimate to the pain, his warrior training had helped him do such things before — he noticed a secondary problem he was dealing with.

His body was shivering as though he'd been thrown naked into twelve feet of snow, and left out overnight.

So cold. So very, very cold. Except for his skull, which seemed to radiate fiery pain, Cavan was enduring a cold the like of which he'd never experienced before. Cold right down to his very...

...soul.

Oh. Yes. The trap.

The trap had been formed of illusions, yes, but it had also caused Cavan real harm. It could be no other way. The power of a necromancer lay in death, and every spell he worked carried a touch of death to it.

That was the power and the limitation of necromancy. A fact that Cavan was amazed he could recall while suffering such pain. But perhaps it was a statement about the life that Cavan lived that, even while enduring pains that would render unconscious — or even slay — a lesser man, Cavan was still capable of functioning on some level.

And Cavan kept his focus on necromancy. On what he could remember of it. The focus kept him sane through the seeming years or decades before the blinding pain in his skull settled down to an aching throb.

Color returned to his world then. Sound as well. Cavan was even able to begin to recognize the world about him.

He yet lay in that clearing, but he'd been covered over with a blanket — though the blanket did little good against the soul-deep chill his body tried to fight — and his head lay in Reesa's lap.

Reesa. Beautiful, worried, Reesa, stroking Cavan's sweaty brow and saying soft little nothings about how she was here, and how she would be here. That Cavan was all right. Everyone was here with him, and they would find a way to make it all right.

Finally, Cavan managed a shaky smile at her, and Reesa called out, "Ehren! He's conscious."

Ehren was there in a flash, with Amra and Qalas watching over his shoulders.

"Spell fire," Ehren said, stroking Cavan's forehead and checking his eyes. "Nod if I'm right."

Cavan managed to direct his shaking in the vague shape of a nod.

"Thought so," Ehren said, giving Cavan a rare frown. "You really must warn us when you're about to do something you aren't prepared for."

"D-D-D-Don't a-a-a-a-al—"

"You don't always know," Ehren said, grimacing now.

A frown *and* a grimace. Must have been really bad.

"All the same," Ehren continued, "you must warn us before you attempt anything you think *might* be too much for you. I really don't relish seeing you suffer this way."

Cavan tried to nod again.

"The cold is different, isn't it?" Amra said, her voice comfortingly matter-of-fact. "He isn't usually so shaky."

"Yes," Ehren said, then began passing his hands in the air above Cavan. "If you can add anything here, it would be appreciated."

"T-T-T-T-T-r-r- r-r—"

"Trap?" Amra asked, and Cavan shook through another nod.

"Great," Ehren said flatly, then blanched. Given how pale the priest usually was, the blanch was an impressive sight. He got nearly as white as his clothes. "Necromancy. Something drained your soul?"

Cavan tried to shrug, but it didn't work. "M-M-M-May—"

"Can't be sure, I know," Ehren said, then turned and dug through his backpack.

"The first rays of the sun would be best for this," he said, and hearing him say "sun" without saying something like "Zatafa's glory" just made Cavan worry about what shape he really was in.

"But," Ehren continued, "this sort of problem is not unknown to me. It's rare, even for us — and I'd like to keep it that way, you understand — but there is a treatment."

Cavan had to close his eyes then. The sun was high overhead, and its brightness was painful. And to be honest, all of his bones were aching from the cold he endured. It was all he could do to keep his teeth from clattering and risk them breaking.

So Cavan tried to focus on his shuddering breaths. Tried to find a way to gather himself, despite the suffering he endured. A true warrior would be able to do it. A true wizard would have done it as soon as he'd returned to his body.

But this was too much. Cavan had no focus. He could barely even keep his attention on the sight of Reesa's pretty gray eyes and the worried way her brow drew together.

But Ehren was praying in rapid Penthix. And Cavan, he didn't smell smoke, quite, but he did smell flame. He tried to sit up, but Ehren held him down with strong hands, and all the while praying.

Then, Cavan felt the queerest sensation of his life. Even stranger than the cold that seemed to radiate from the very core of his self.

Within that core, Cavan felt a flicker. Light. Heat.

Whatever it was didn't catch. It faded.

But then it came again. And again. And each time it came back stronger. Each time, Ehren's voice got louder. Clearer.

Cavan would have even sworn that Ehren's words seemed to echo inside him.

Finally, the spark caught. Then, within the frozen region deep inside Cavan, it was as though a tiny stream of flame worked its way up and down, up and down. From down past the soles of his feet to up past his head.

Swift now, slow now, but always moving. And each pass made the flame a little brighter. A little warmer. A little wider.

Sooner than Cavan dared dream, the heat replaced the cold, and he once again felt enough like himself to reach up and kiss Reesa.

Reesa made a small sound of surprise, but gave herself to the kiss, holding Cavan to herself every bit as tight as Cavan held her.

"All right, all right," Amra said after a moment. "I presume you discovered something more than the need for a kiss?"

Cavan broke the kiss and gave a smile that included all of them, and a nod of thanks for Ehren, who would not have willingly listened to more gratitude than that as he gathered up the candles he'd lit and placed, one by Cavan's feet and the other by his head.

Reesa was smiling back, which just made Cavan feel all the better as he stood, then held her hand as she rose from her kneeling position.

"Oh, I've learned quite a bit. And we need to get moving."

Despite the urgency Cavan felt to get riding, he had one more spell to cast before he could leave the clearing.

The trap he had encountered was sprung and gone. Nothing remained of it. However. That horrific rite he'd witnessed, that had been a powerful spell. Powerful enough that its echoes had reverberated into the very surroundings.

If Cavan could gather the proper remnants of that spell, he could link those remnants to their caster, no matter how much time had passed since that fateful night.

Not a strong link, true, but enough for what he needed.

First, Cavan went to the largest of the trees that formed the innermost ring around the clearing.

He placed both hands upon that tree. Whispered softly, hoping that he had the words right. He spoke little of the language of the walking trees, but had been assured that all trees understood it.

"I have need," he whispered, or intended, at the least. *"To undo a horrible wrong done in this place. A wrong we both witnessed, though only one of us was there at the time. A wrong worse than fire among saplings. Would you aid me with a twig?"*

A small branch fell from above to land at Cavan's feet. Cavan had only been hoping for a twig. Perhaps something as thick as a finger and long as his hand. What he got was as thick as his wrist and long as his forearm, with smaller twigs still full of needles.

"Thank you," Cavan said, confident that he had *those* words right, at least.

Cavan stripped away the smaller twigs and needles, and left them at the foot of the donating tree.

Then, trusting to what his wizard sight had told him earlier, he stepped across the clearing to the spot where the vermilion aura was strongest. Yes, he could have seen it again, had he chosen, but having fallen into one trap today, Cavan had no desire to discover that he'd overlooked another only to stumble into it.

At that spot, he dug in the dirt for a small stone. Tied it to the end of the branch with a strip of leather. Then rubbed the stone and leather with dirt from the same spot.

"Rass ka, neel ne atacha," Cavan intoned the incantation while flaring the right amount of power across the end of the branch.

Pain followed the flare of power, but that would be true every time Cavan used magic between now and ... likely sunset. Possibly the next sunrise. Pain that was the price of overreaching himself earlier, and one Cavan was more than willing to pay right then.

Violet, heatless flame sprang up from the end of the branch.

Flame that immediately leaned toward the northeast, confirming what Cavan had concluded earlier.

"The flame will point the way to the necromancer," Cavan said, smiling through the ache in his head. "And now, it is time to ride."

Riding felt glorious after all Cavan had been through that day. To have Dzint beneath him, open land stretching out before him, and his friends all around him, riding to right a wrong.

Truly, one of the best feelings Cavan knew.

Alas, he did not get to savor it quite so much as he would have wished. He had tales to tell and questions to answer.

Three times, in fact, Cavan had to repeat the tale of what he had witnessed during his spell. Three times, as he and his friends rode slowly northeast out of the woods and across rolling hills of goldenrod in the afternoon sunshine.

Each time, though Cavan's report was essentially the same, someone had different questions that required going through it all again, in detail.

And each time, they asked about things Cavan considered less important than what he had observed about the necromancer himself.

Amra had asked questions about the risen dead. How they moved. What order they moved in. If there seemed to be any traces of their past selves in their mannerisms.

Cavan, of course, could not have spoken to such traces, as he had known none of these men and women in life. But he repeated what he had seen, because facts were clearer to Amra than even half a wizard's conclusions.

Cavan felt certain that the spirits had been bound with the bodies. Ehren, at least, understood what that meant to the same degree that Cavan did, albeit likely along different lines.

Cavan, of course, considered the magical implications of that fact. Ehren, no doubt, took a religious angle.

And always Amra stayed on the military side of the street. Oh, it was true she'd grown more philosophical over the past year, but not so much that it deviated her from concerns over planning and tactics.

Either way, Cavan's observations meant that Amra should count on those "traces" of personality remaining. Which, as she explained, meant the knights would retain a sense of tactics, and ability to coordinate their fighting. Something to guard against.

She would have had Cavan go through several more recitations, had he let her, in order to ensure he had missed nothing. And under normal circumstances, that would have been a good idea.

Usually, describing what he saw to his friends brought questions that made Cavan realize he'd seen even more of what he'd observed than he would have believed beforehand.

But this time Cavan's observations had come through a spell. And the nature of observation through magic was such that it followed attention.

Details missed the first time were not witnessed and present to be recovered through memory. They were simply missed. However much Amra refused to believe that.

Ehren, of course, had wanted more details on the seven-pointed star, and everything Cavan could recall about the mannerisms of the rising corpses. Though what Ehren would conclude from this information, Cavan could not begin to guess.

Qalas' questions, at least, had not required another recitation. But then, Qalas had been more focused on the archer, and Cavan had seen no signs of the archer. Not even so much as the shadow of anyone alive near the clearing, save the necromancer, nor any sign of the archer among the risen dead.

Qalas concluded that Cavan's not seeing the archer meant the archer was indeed working for the necromancer. Otherwise, the necromancer would likely have killed the archer, and raised him along with the others.

A valid point, in Cavan's opinion, and one he considered unusual. What would a necromancer want with a living servant? Why would anyone with life in their veins choose to serve a necromancer?

At least this was a topic for speculation that carried the conversation away from forcing Cavan to relive what he had witnessed.

Still, Cavan felt good again, after the horrible pains and cold he'd experienced. And he was riding his blue roan hobby again, with his friends around him and a task before him.

Yes, they were riding into the hazard. And yes, Reesa was untried in anything more than a duel, so far as Cavan knew.

But he had to take his pleasures in life where he could find them. And right there, right then, riding in good company as he was.

Life was good.

THE FOREST OF RISEN KNIGHTS. LEAVE IT TO A NECROMANCER TO NAME a forest after his own work.

But what did Vastig care about the name of any forest? No forest welcomed him. Not anymore.

Even this tiny speck of woods. This copse. This grove. This nothing compared to the mighty Wailing Woods that he had known in his youth, his glory, and his shame.

Even these *neelach* trees dared grumble at Vastig as he strode between them, heading for the clearing he needed. Little reminders that, no matter how small the grove, no trees would aid him ever again.

For most forest elves, banishment meant death. But, as Vastig had learned, death need not be the end.

The clearing looked much as he remembered it, though he had not been here since the night that gave these woods their name.

How long ago was that now? Five years? Ten? Who bothered keeping count?

The trees themselves, of course, had aged in ways he could not help but notice. They grew, and they spread their roots and seeds, so that, given enough time and food, this little bit of a copse might become impressive.

Vastig was tempted to burn it down, rather than see that happen.

But no. The necromancer would not stand for it. Anyplace he renamed for his deeds had to stand in eternal tribute to his work.

Someone, however, had disturbed *this* tribute. Vastig could see that even as he entered the clearing.

There had been a fire here, just this very morning. An encampment. Human, to judge not only by the lingering smell — fainter than Vastig expected for traveling humans — and experienced at covering their tracks.

Poor humans. Little did they likely realize they did not need to hide their movements from one of their own kind, but from a forest elf. And even a disgraced forest elf knew more of hunting than a human could learn in a dozen lifetimes.

And this particular forest elf, disgraced though he might be, had learned even more about hunting humanoids over the last several decades.

So Vastig had no trouble determining that five humans had camped here overnight. They'd had some sort of disturbance — no doubt whatever they did to trigger the master's trap — and yet had seen the night through, and not left with the first rays of dawn.

Why would that be? Were any of them injured? Did they have healers?

Interesting.

Vastig went over and over the clearing. Once upon a time, he could have asked the trees about those who had camped here. At the time, he considered this a wondrous gift.

Now, he knew it for the crutch it was. Vastig needed no trees to tell him what he could gather from his senses.

Five humans, with horses. Three hobbies, a rouncey, and a courser. The hobbies moved as though they had been raised together, trained together.

Then three of them were companions. Likely escorting the other two.

Vastig felt certain that two of the humans had romantic intentions towards each other. They must have been the ones escorted. Nobles perhaps, or rich enough to hire guards and live the way they wished, rather than whatever tradition would have demanded of them.

The other three must have been warriors then. Two of them were,

Vastig was certain, and one was quite experienced to have cleared away the campsite as well as they had.

Most human efforts were so paltry that Vastig could have determined not only what the humans ate last night — roast chicken with vegetables in this case — but also what they had eaten for the three nights before. Perhaps even where they had camped the night before, as well.

But Vastig could not deduce as much as he expected, and this pleased him. There might be a challenge in this hunt after all.

Once they began riding, the humans did not cover their tracks. They made no effort to disguise that they were riding...

Northeast?

Truly?

They escaped the necromancer's trap, and now they rode in his direction?

Or could that be coincidence?

Vastig banished all conclusions from his mind. Returned to the clearing and hunted for the signs of the direction the humans had ridden to *arrive* in the clearing.

That took some time. They had covered those tracks, for some reason, though they had not covered their path out. Why?

Someone thought they might be followed. But that someone was not given time to prevent it.

Or that someone *wanted* to be followed. More interesting still.

In any event, Vastig determined before too long that the humans had been riding north by northwest when they came to the woods. That meant that northeast was definitely a departure. There could be no other conclusion then.

They had encountered the necromancer's trap, eluded it, and sought payback.

Oh, this hunt might prove fun.

Alas, though, if they were all mounted, then Vastig could not risk the time lag of following on foot. He would have no choice. He would have to ride.

From his belt, Vastig pulled a section of antler no longer than his smallfinger. It was taken from Lasitasanathila, the great elk who had once been his prized mount.

Vastig left the clearing and those damnable, muttering woods by the quickest route, still on foot.

Then, by the light of the late afternoon sun, he tossed down the carved-off bit of elk antler, and said the words he hated saying.

"Shul na keena a sakath, Lasitasanathila."

The section of antler began to shiver. Hopped around, there in the dirt, among trampled down goldenrod.

Then the antler grew longer. Formed once again the section of rack it had been carved away from. Still, it hopped about.

Then from the section of rack, a skull.

The rest of the rack filled in, and then the spine began to grow. Then the ribs, the legs, and the rest of the skeleton, until it stood before him, regarding Vastig with those vacant eye sockets. Once more Vastig felt judgment from those sockets, blame for the state that had befallen one of the great elks of the Wailing Woods.

Once Vastig's truest friend. Now, merely a collection of bones animated to carry him about, when speed was needed.

One of the necromancer's little jokes. A perpetual reminder that Vastig himself was just a set of bones and flesh, waiting for his master's spells on the day he ceased being useful.

Vastig mounted the skeletal elk, and rode off to ensure that that day would not be *this* day.

It was Amra who chose their campsite for the night.

Oh, she let Cavan or Qalas do it sometimes, but whenever she felt that they might be under threat, she inevitably insisted on choosing where they camped.

And Cavan had to admit, she knew better than he did.

Amra had managed to find the crest of a hill with a good distance of visibility around it, north of the path of the rainfall. Most of what surrounded the hill were fields of goldenrod, but a few lower hills and occasional clumps of underbrush of one sort or another, that Ehren suggested indicated places an underground stream neared the surface.

Their encampment even had a trio of rocks big enough to hide the tracking torch, which would continue to burn with its heatless violet flame pointing the way to the necromancer.

The campsite had good visibility, by the dying light of day. Of course, its elevation meant that Ehren was practically on a stage when he offered up his sunset prayers.

Qalas, as usual, watched Ehren's prayers with his head bowed. Reesa surprised Cavan by joining Ehren in the recitation. Which meant either she actually spoke some ancient Penthix, or had at least learned the words phonetically.

Cavan hadn't known that about her.

"Careful," Amra said. She stood next to him, as the two of them finished rubbing down the horses and preparing them for the evening.

The horses would be bedded down in the center of camp tonight. A night without a fire, because, as Amra had said, there was no reason to *invite* trouble they weren't already expecting.

This time she'd even foregone the words she usually finished that saying with: apart, of course, from the joy of it.

But Cavan was more interested in the point Amra was raising right now.

"Careful about what?" he asked, finishing his brushing of Dzint's coat, and moving on to Highsun, while Amra continued with Caramel.

"This is no time to fall in love, you idiot."

She at least had the decency to keep her voice low. As though they could have been heard over the evening prayers to Zatafa.

"I'm not," Cavan said, though the roiling in his stomach might have been more than hunger from the ride.

"Make sure you keep it that way." She wasn't even looking at him now, her full attention seemingly on her task. "What happens to a warrior whose focus splits during a battle?"

"The same thing that would happen to a wizard, I expect."

Amra turned and gave Cavan a flat look. "Exactly."

"There's no point in worrying about it anyway," Cavan said. "I don't even—"

"There's no point because it's foolish. Once we survive this, then you can figure out if you want to go back to Juno and set up your household with her. Or if she wants to ride the world with us, assuming she's good enough. Or whatever other options there might be."

Amra turned then. "But, Cavan, remember something." She waited until Cavan faced her. "You might not be more to this girl than a pleasant time in the sheets and a way out from under her father's tyranny."

Cavan frowned.

Amra smiled. "Hadn't occurred to you, had it?" She chuckled and shook her head. "You men. You think you're the only ones who can tumble someone without giving away your heart."

Cavan snorted. "No one who rides with *you* could possibly believe that."

Amra chuckled, unabashed, and let Cavan return to his thoughts as they finished with the horses.

Was Amra right? Could Reesa really be preparing to give Cavan a speech about what she wasn't looking for?

Cavan, who didn't know himself what *he* was looking for?

He tried not to think on this overmuch as they all dined on dried strips of beef, apples, and hardtack from Reesa's saddlebags. Her idea, rather than letting it go to waste.

Cavan even tried not to pay too much attention to Reesa as they all settled toward their bedrolls for the evening.

But his thoughts kept circling the subject all the same. Right up until the moment he stood to cast the warding he cast every night while they traveled. *Especially* when they were in an area that might prove dangerous.

"Stop," Ehren said, the moment Cavan stood.

Cavan frowned at his smiling friend, his teeth still visible in the light of the rising gibbous moon. But the certainty in those clear blue eyes could not be denied.

"What?" Cavan said. "I was just going to—"

"Lie down until it's your turn to stand watch," Ehren said, his voice as firm as though he were giving Cavan a medical treatment.

"But—"

"But nothing," Ehren said, his smiling never budging an inch. "You're not recovered from that little experiment of yours this morning, are you?"

"I think I am," Cavan said, then frowned, trying to suss out the truth of his statement without attempting the kind of stimulus that would answer the question once and for all.

"You forget," Ehren said. "I've been present every time you've dealt with spell fire in the last several years. Do you think for one instant that I haven't studied the effects on you?"

Cavan knew better than to answer that. But Ehren wasn't done talking anyway.

"You, my friend, will not be recovered before the dawn. *Possibly* not until highsun tomorrow, though I don't think you'll need that long. I think the night's sleep will do it."

"Then—"

"*Assuming*," Ehren said, still smiling, "I don't let you do something stupid like cast another spell before then, and risk hurting yourself further."

"But—"

"I'll grant you," Ehren continued, "your tracking torch *was* absolutely necessary. Time is of the essence for us. But wards tonight?"

Ehren shook his head.

"May I speak?"

"Will you say something worth hearing?" Amra asked, and Cavan didn't have to look at her to know she was fluttering her eyelashes.

"The warding I cast each night is a simple spell. One I know better than nearly any other, and can cast with great efficiency. There is no need for this concern."

"There is no need for you to cast it and do yourself even that little bit of harm." Ehren shook his head. "I say it's watches tonight. Any more spells from you, Cavan, will wait for the dawn."

"I concur," Amra said.

"Me too," Qalas said. "Truth is, I kind of miss keeping watch. It's peaceful."

"Unless it isn't," Amra added, a grin all through her voice.

"I don't know what my opinion counts for in this," Reesa said, a little steel in her own voice, despite her words, "but I agree. No suffering you don't *have* to endure."

She directed her next words to Amra.

"And I'll keep watch for a shift as well."

"Have you ever done it before?" Amra asked.

"No, but—"

"Then you can't stand watch alone yet. You'll watch with me tonight, and I'll teach you how to do it right." Amra clapped her hands once and pitched her next words in her command voice. "That's decided. The rest of you sack out. I'll wake Qalas for second watch."

At least Cavan's irritation gave him something else to think about as he fell asleep.

Some sudden loud cry yanked Cavan from his sleep.

He lay in his bedroll, his head pounding and his eyes heavy. He must have only just gotten into the deepest part of sleep before...

...before what? Why was he...

"Ware! Archers!" Amra called again, and the world snapped into focus.

Cavan rolled to his knees. Slipped into his *licha* hauberk and leggings. Grabbed his sword belt and buckled it on before standing. His feet were still bare, but he'd fought that way before.

Amra stood near the edge of their encampment. Sword naked in her hand.

Reesa crouched behind her, longbow ready and an arrow knocked.

"I see no movement," Reesa said. "But the moonlight doesn't—"

"Ehren!" Amra called, and just like that Ehren was there, offering up the prayer that would turn the darkest tunnel into bright daylight.

The prayer shed no light, and cast no shadows. It only granted the vision of Zatafa's brilliance to the eyes of those whom Her priest blessed this way.

And just that fast, Cavan could see far into the distance, in any direction he chose, as though it were a cloudless midday.

Reesa gasped, then started muttering what sounded like prayers in praise of Zatafa.

Qalas already studied the lands in the opposite direction from Amra's facing, so Cavan alternated between their flanks. Trying to cover both at once.

But Cavan saw nothing larger than a fox moving out there.

"Gone," Amra said quickly. "But the arrow came from this way. I'll pursue."

"Wait," Qalas said.

To Cavan's surprise, she did.

"You know as well as I do it could be a trap," Qalas said, maintaining his watch. "You indicate it came from the nearest hill. How would *you* take you out?"

"I'd have archers hidden and ready for pursuit to come," Amra grumbled, "with shots aimed from multiple directions at once, figuring even I couldn't dodge or parry all of them."

"Exactly," Qalas said.

"Just as well, I suppose," Amra said, frowning as she crouched and picked up a shattered arrow. "This is forest elf work. Tells us pretty much everything we need to know, wouldn't you say?"

"How?" Reesa said. "How does that tell us *everything we need to know? How did you cut that arrow out of midair?*"

"As to the second," Amra said, her voice more full of patience than Cavan expected, "I didn't. I blocked it with the flat of my blade. As to the first, Simple." Amra shrugged. "In fact, I'll let Cavan explain it. I'm not *positive* this assault is over. If I were planning it, it wouldn't be."

"Chances are strong," Cavan said, while Amra began checking other sight lines, "that whoever shot that arrow is the same archer who shot at the knights and raiders, back in that clearing. Confirms that he or she is working for the necromancer, and now likely tasked with trying to stop us before we *reach* the necromancer. Or, to be more precise, kill us and bring certain parts of us back to his or her master."

"If I may," Qalas said, and waited for Cavan's nod before he continued, to Reesa. "You might be thinking that it's possible that this is a human archer, working with forest elf arrows, or that the attack is unrelated. First, however, no human is likely to have tried that shot. Not without support."

"Why?" Reesa asked.

"You're an archer, would you have tried it? All on your own?"

Reesa frowned and eyed the distance. Turned and looked over the group assembled around her on the hilltop. Shook her head. "It's suicide. Even if I hit my target, I couldn't have gotten you all before you caught me. Not working with only moonlight, and all of you coming, and—"

"Just so. And while I can't deny we have other enemies — especially Cavan, who seems to collect them the way a bard collects rumors — it's safe to say any of our established enemies would do more than fire a single arrow at us. And what else could it be? Bandits? Shooting only a single arrow, and not rushing us?"

Qalas waited until Reesa shook her head, then said, "This shot was as much a test as anything else. Cavan? You want to continue? You know the forest elves better than I do."

"Forest elves see as well at night as we do by day, so the darkness doesn't give them pause. Also, it's a safer shot for a forest elf, because you'll never track a forest elf on foot in terrain like this. Can't happen. They're not capable of leaving a trail in damn near any environment where you're likely to meet one. Just about the only places a forest elf will leave a footprint are in snow or sand."

"Ice elves, and dune elves," Reesa said, thoughtfully.

"Exactly," Cavan said, with a nod. "Most of the land around here suits forest elves far more than any of the other varieties. A battalion of forest elves could march by us and leave no sign of their passage."

"So a human would fight the darkness and risk being caught if he missed, but for a forest elf it was a safe shot. No risk."

"More than that," Qalas said. "It was a way to test us. Gauge our response. If the shot struck and caused chaos in our camp, the archer likely gets at least one or two more good shots before it became time to leave."

"We could have all died?" Reesa looked a little sick.

"Missed that one," Amra said, eyes still scanning. "We're not just anyone."

"I'm starting to really understand that," Reesa muttered, but whatever she was going to say next was lost to Amra's next words.

"Definitely gone," Amra said. "Even forest elves aren't *that* good at hiding away from their trees. I say we check it out."

"Will anyone get angry at me if I cast a spell?" Cavan asked.

"Right now? Yes," Ehren said. "If we run into trouble and it becomes necessary, I'll overlook it. This time."

"Gee," Cavan started, but Qalas interrupted.

"One of us needs to stay here. Watch the camp. Just in case the backup goal is to take out our horses."

"More than one," Ehren said. "You and I will stay. Reesa? You should as well."

"I want one archer with me, just in case," Amra said. "I'm not giving up my sword for a bow right now."

Cavan opened his mouth to speak.

"Please," Amra said. "Don't embarrass yourself. You throw daggers pretty well, but you're useless with arrows and you aren't casting anything unless you have no choice. Reesa, you're with us too."

Reesa nodded, determination all through her features again.

Amra took the lead. Then Reesa. Cavan followed last. He and Amra had their swords in hand. Reesa kept an arrow ready, but her bowstring not drawn. Cavan thought he heard her muttering little encouragements to herself, under her breath.

Amra led the way down their hill and up the next, directly to a short, wide flat rock on that hill. Perfect for hiding behind, if an archer could crouch low enough.

"Damn it," Amra said, scuffing the bottom of her boot as she kicked across the rock. "How did I not spot this? I might as well have said, 'Here archer, have a perfect hidey hole.'"

"Hardly perfect," Reesa said. "You spotted him right away."

"No," Amra said, one finger raised to make her point. "I spotted him *after* he shot. That's as useless as never spotting him at all."

"No sign he was ever here," Cavan said. "Definitely a forest elf then."

"Missed one," Amra said, pointing to something down the hill. Even with Ehren's blessing lighting the way, Cavan couldn't tell what he'd missed from where he stood.

Amra trotted down the hill, eyes scanning the horizon. Cavan followed next this time, with Reesa bringing up the rear.

"Look at the tracks," Amra said, pointing. "Are they what I think they are?"

The tracks were made by the hooves of a four-legged creature. Split like they were left by an elk, but immense. As for an elk whose shoulders stood higher than Cavan's head.

But they didn't dent the dirt as deeply as they should have...

"Great elk tracks," Cavan said. "Lighter than they should be, but there aren't any other good options. Nothing else in this region leaves a hoofprint nearly that big."

"Don't forest elves use great elks as mounts?" Reesa asked, her tone only a little wistful.

"They do," Amra confirmed.

"Tracks lead in, but not away," Cavan said.

"So where did the elk go?" Amra asked, finishing the thought. "Ideas?"

"None at the moment," Cavan said, looking up. "Unless you think it took wing."

The question was meant in jest, but Amra took it seriously.

"I'd've seen it, and so would Reesa."

"Forest elf magic?" Reesa asked.

Amra looked at Cavan.

"Never heard of forest elves being able to hide their elk tracks, but I suppose they could have..." Cavan shook his head. "No. If I could hide Dzint's hoofprints, I'd do it on approach to my target, as well as on escape."

"Otherwise you'd risk your enemy learning of the capability for no useful gain," Amra said, eyes still scanning. "I agree."

"So what happened to the elk then?" Reesa asked.

"No idea," Cavan said, "and that troubles me."

———

BRISK, COOL NIGHT AIR FOR A LONG RUN UNDER A WANING GIBBOUS moon.

Vastig should have recalled Lasitasanathila by now. Should be riding across these hills, instead of running. He knew that. His master would expect him to return with all speed, given what he had gleaned from his investigation. And he had covered more than enough ground to ensure that mere humans could not follow him.

But excitement burned through Vastig's veins. Pounded his heart.

Who could ride, after seeing what he'd seen?

The arrow shot had been perfect. Timed for the moment that woman, that *human*, looked away in response to something said by her companion. The one who held a bow as though she believed she could use it.

Perfect timing. Perfect angle. Perfect arc. Perfect speed.

Perfect.

It should have slain the dark-haired woman. The fair-haired woman should have turned, puzzled by her companion's collapse, raised her excuse for a bow ... and fallen silent to an arrow in the throat.

The other three humans had been sleeping, or near enough to it.

They would never have mounted a defense before three more arrows added them to Vastig's larder.

Slaughtering the five of them should have been a simple matter. Vastig should have been feasting even now.

But that was not how events unfolded.

It *should* have been. Vastig had made no mistakes. Given away no signs. He was sure of it. Not when he took up his position. Not when he called up that concealing stone from within the hill. He had even held back from loosing his intended second shot, knowing to wait for the result of his first arrow.

That dark-haired woman could have seen *nothing*. She could have heard *nothing*. She could not possibly have known even that Vastig was nearby, let alone that he had fired an arrow toward her back, aiming for the heart.

And yet...

And *yet...*

Her parry was exquisite. That strange, dark sword of hers, interposed exactly in time to catch Vastig's arrow. Precisely enough strength to the movement that the blade did not so much as twitch when the arrow struck.

Not just struck. *Shattered*.

No human warrior had instincts that good. No human female could have had the strength that parry showed. Vastig could draw only one conclusion.

That was no ordinary sword.

Only a *highly* enchanted blade could have warned her. Could have ensured that it interposed itself between harm and its wielder.

The woman with the sword. She might be nothing on her own. Just another arrogant human, believing her scant collection of skirmishes made her an expert in the field of war. Arrogant enough not to respect the true warriors, who had survived their battles for *centuries*.

But that sword.

Marvelous. Wondrous. The work of a master.

Vastig would claim it from her corpse. She parried one arrow, yes, but even the mightiest of swords would need a true warrior's hand to handle as many arrows as Vastig could loose in the span of a breath.

Or, for that matter, to handle him in melee, where he would whirl with his blades until he'd sliced her to ribbons.

Even the swords of the ancient, lost Dunaians could be in only one place at a time. Could not defend the throat, while guarding the stomach.

Oh, yes. Vastig would slay this woman and claim her blade. Two-handed, which was less than ideal, but it would still likely prove superior to even the best *zil* swords he had ever seen.

In Vastig's hands, that sword would mean *revenge*.

But he needed a plan. No sword that powerful would surrender its wielder's life easily. It had already proven as much. So long as that woman had her friends about her and that sword in her hands, she was all too dangerous.

But the necromancer, he could make the difference here. He wouldn't care about the sword, but he would have his own interests in this little group.

One of the humans had enough aura that he probably fancied himself a mighty wizard. Had to have been the one to have stumbled into the necromancer's trap, and eluded it through sheer luck.

He could only have escaped through luck, because he lacked the power to burst his way out. And since power and skill were one, luck was the only explanation.

Another of the humans looked to be a priest of their sun goddess. The master would enjoy that one even more than he'd likely enjoy the would-be wizard.

Sun gods tended to hate the undead, so their priests were prizes.

That left three. The sword-wielder, the would-be archer, and ... another warrior. Possibly decent. Difficult to judge while he slept. He did use a halberd, so he couldn't be all that good, even among humans.

Everyone knew that the weapon of a true warrior was the sword.

Yes, Vastig would return to his master. Report what he had seen, and the direction they rode. Explain that they yet lived because Vastig carried only enough preservative for one heart and one skull, which meant either the wizard or the priest would be lost.

The necromancer would accept this reason as sound judgment. He would consult with Vastig about the best ways to deal with them.

They would plan.

They would strike.

Vastig would claim for his own what could only be a mighty relic. And then, revenge would be his.

Soon.

7

————

WHILE EVERYONE AGREED THAT THE FOREST ELF ARCHER WAS GONE, Amra insisted that another attack might be coming. Cavan wasn't sure about that, but he agreed that the safest play was to assume it would, and not be there when it came.

Thus, Cavan and his friends broke camp and rode for an hour due east under a starry sky. Ehren's prayers lit the way for both riders and horses, without shedding so much as a visible candlelight for any observing enemies to see.

Cavan kept the heatless violet tracking torch burning, concealed within his cloak, so that even that light would not be visible.

If anyone, indeed, was watching.

They settled once more on another hilltop. Took some time to choose the right one, for they were finding more copses of those unusual evergreens, and they all agreed that camping near trees would be giving any forest elves in the area an unfair advantage.

They finally lay out their camp sometime before midnight, on a low hill that managed to be taller than any near it, among greener grasses, and weeds that Cavan knew produced a crunchy kind of berry the local orcs liked to cook with.

This time, Amra and Qalas checked the surrounding hilltops to ensure that no good hiding spots for an archer had gone overlooked.

Thus satisfied, the group bedded down for the remainder of the night, with Qalas standing the next watch, before waking Cavan for the watch that would see them to dawn.

Ehren had actually started to argue that, until Cavan reminded the smiling priest of his tendency toward predawn sleepiness.

Oh, Ehren wasn't *useless* at night, but he was never at his best either.

At least the attack had accomplished one good thing for Cavan. It had distracted his thoughts from … unproductive lines. He'd been able to return to sleep easily enough, after the ride, and now that he stood watch, his focus was right where it should have been.

Awareness.

He noted every change in the cool, late night breeze. More importantly, that it carried the scent of goldenrod and fresh dirt, as well as the pungent scent of those weed berries, but not any signs of other horses, or worse, great elk.

Though Ehren's sunlight vision prayer had faded when the smiling priest went back to sleep, the light of the gibbous moon was more than enough to keep Cavan aware of any nearby movement larger than a field mouse or vole.

He considered extending his vision into wizard sight, but Ehren was right. The less he attempted, the sooner he would recover from the spell fire.

Besides. If an attack came from the necromancer, Cavan would still sense it. Necromancy was hardly the subtlest form of magic.

Still, all was quiet, here among the hills. The distant swoop of an owl. The flutter of a bat. The bark of a hunting fox. These were Cavan's only companions on watch that night.

They were good company, and helped keep his focus right where it needed to be throughout a watch that was the kind of quiet Cavan needed.

Focused quiet. It had healing qualities of its own, and it would give the back of his mind time to worry at ... other matters while his attention stayed where it belonged.

His watch passed without incident, and Cavan found himself in the rare position of being the one to wake others for the morning.

Well, the one to wake Reesa. The other three woke easily enough on their own, as the dawn neared.

Reesa, though, was not used to this life. Even in her sleep, her brow looked troubled, and Cavan had to shake her twice before her eyes snapped open and she gasped.

"Arrows?" she said. "Archers?"

"You're safe," Cavan said, empty hands raised in a calming gesture. "It's morning."

To her credit, she laughed away her chagrin.

Soon they'd broken their fast of more of Reesa's trail rations of dried beef, hard bread, and cheese, along with fresh spring water from Ehren's backpack. No workouts this morning. Chances were, there'd be no need. They'd face real combat again soon enough.

The dawn broke and Ehren greeted it with songs and prayers, with Reesa joining in.

Finally, once more, they rode north. Well, north by northwest was Cavan's estimate. But Amra was in the lead, and she held the tracking torch for the time being.

The hills began to flatten, and the green of the grasses faded to gold as they rode. Trees became fewer. And as midday approached, when the wind shifted to come down from the north, it lacked the sort of healthy, growing smells they'd grown used to.

The smell wasn't dead. It was just ... wrong. Sick. Not merely decay, but a foulness underneath that decay.

Amra whistled the three-note trill that halted all the horses except Horizon, who had not undergone the training the others had been put to.

Amra's raised hand was enough signal for Reesa to rein in.

"What do you think?" Amra asked Ehren. "A plaguemaster's work?"

Plaguemasters. Priests of Kulath the Pestilence. One of the foulest gods Cavan could name — or rather, was *willing* to. Certainly, the smell seemed to Cavan as though it might be...

"No," Ehren said with a firm shake of his head. "I've had the misfortune to smell the handiwork of the Pestilence's priests, and we would already be gagging from the stench."

"All the same," Amra said, "we should back off a bit and take one more break for the horses, before we continue. I don't relish the idea of our horses grazing anywhere that can smell like that."

No arguments, of course, but urgency had them back in the saddle and moving as soon as they reasonably could. Though it helped the horses that they were riding even slower than their usual long-distance pace.

The hobbies would have been only too happy to hold a quicker pace throughout a long day's ride, but Qalas' rouncey lacked their stamina, as likely did Reesa's courser. Though they would not be certain that was true of Horizon unless they tested it. But it seemed to Cavan a likely guess.

Even at that slower pace, they had not been riding long before the reason for the growing stench became clear.

Cavan and his friends halted atop a low hill without the need for whistles or signals. Not with the sight they beheld from where they stopped.

The land ... changed ahead of them. Exactly halfway down a hill.

———

Cavan and his friends sat ahorse atop a low hill, under a warm, midday sun. What clouds littered the sky above were white, though some toward the horizon were the darker grays of rain clouds.

The sky should not be so beautiful. Not here. It was *wrong* that they should see such a sight as the land that lay before them, smell such a rank odor as assailed their nostrils, under a high, beautiful sun and sky.

Such sights and smells as these should have been restricted to late nights. Moonless nights. Cursed nights.

Because the land ahead of them could only have been cursed.

The others might not see that yet, but Cavan did.

The top of this hill, this last hill, was fine. A mixture of green and golden grasses, a sight that continued down the hill just about exactly halfway.

There, everything changed.

The grasses ahead were gnarled, and a sickly shade of yellowish brown. Where the grasses at the top of the hill grew beyond ankle height, those sickened grasses ahead would barely crest a handspan. Had Cavan been confident enough of the ground to test their height.

He was not that confident in the ground. Had no desire to touch it.

Here atop the hill, the ground was not the rich dark loam of good farming — the summer had been too dry through here for that — but it still had a good, reddish brown hue, even in the places it cracked from the heat of days past.

But down the hill, the ground was black like squid ink, with dark red undertones. As though blood had soaked into it to the point Cavan half-wondered if Dzint's hooves would squish when he rode ahead.

And the ground lacked the ... granularity of proper dirt. It was smooth, like rubbed clay.

Lone trees dotted that sick land ahead of them. Twisted things, lacking leaves even this early in the year. What bark they had was the yellow of old bones, and cracked and peeled all across the trunks of those trees.

"Ehren was right," Cavan said, his voice hushed as though he spoke near the dying. "This isn't the work of a plaguemaster."

"What makes you so sure?" Qalas asked. "That land looks plague-ridden to me."

Cavan pointed down the hill, to the transition point. The place the good, healthy land met the sick, twisted abomination ahead of them.

"See the way it arcs?" Cavan continued pointing off into the distance. "Razor sharp point of change, following the curve of a tremendous circle."

"A spell?" Amra asked in shocked disbelief. "A single spell did all this?"

"The opposite," Cavan said, shaking his head. "An accumulation of perverse magics, spreading their influence from a central point."

"The necromancer," Ehren said.

Cavan nodded. "Powerful and long-entrenched, from the look of this. At least the height of the tracking torch's flame" — three fingers tall now — "says we should reach him by nightfall."

"I don't relish that idea," Qalas said. "I'd rather have Zatafa overhead when we face the necromancer."

"So would we all," Amra said, which got her a raised eye from Ehren. She shot him a lopsided grin. "Don't worry. I'm not becoming a zealot. But I'm not stupid, either."

Ehren, wisely, hid his thoughts behind his smile.

"Any chance this is an elaborate trap?" Amra asked Cavan.

Cavan sighed — which had the misfortune of giving him a lungful of the wretched odors — and enhanced his wizard sight.

"Neela asa."

Cavan caught himself wincing in expectation of the pain of spell fire, but to his relief he had indeed fully recovered. He once again had all his resources available to him.

Now he could see the cause behind the foulness easily enough. Necromancy. The power of death battling the power of life, and slowly ebbing it away from all the natural things between Cavan and the necromancer.

Everything that lived within this domain was battling, just to stay alive. And now Cavan could easily spot the swaths were the fell magics had won the day. Large sections of the grasses and trees were already dead. Though some of them still pretended otherwise.

No single spell to it. But no safe direct path either.

"Necromancy," Cavan said.

"We'll need to bring in a priest of Halstaffur the Green Lord," Ehren said. "Set the land to right."

"We need to kill the necromancer first," Amra said. "Little detail, but important."

"Then it's time to go," Cavan said, urging Dzint forward. Amra rode beside him, and Ehren, Qalas and Reesa rode together in a second rank.

Down the hill they went. Cavan savored the last few strides of his horse across the healthy land they'd been riding...

Cavan was the first to cross the dividing line. And he was the first to breath in the stench of dying air.

"Stale," Amra said. "Like that tomb. Remember? In Traklis?"

As though Cavan could ever forget. The tomb of Rikakan III, a long-dead sorcerer king of Voraas, the kingdom that fell before Traklis rose. Rikakan had laid a curse on the land that held off three centuries before striking. A curse that began to twist and corrupt the children of the kingdom.

Cavan, Ehren and Amra had faced many traps and challenges stalking down into that tomb as they sought a way to undo that curse.

"Not quite the same," Cavan said. "That air was made stale by time and dust. This air, it's as though it's being throttled of its own life."

Cavan called the halt. Led everyone back up to the top of the hill, then down it again onto the healthy side.

"We can't just ride in there like this." He shook his head. "If we spend more than a day breathing air like that, we may not survive it. And the horses definitely wouldn't."

"How can the necromancer survive it?" Reesa asked.

"I don't know if 'survive' is the word I'd choose," Cavan said with a grimace. "Necromancers ... exist in a blend of death and life together."

"But what can we do about the air?" Ehren asked. "Zatafa's glory may smite the undead, but this ... this is outside of Zatafa's purview. And there couldn't be a priest of the Green Lord anywhere near this place. They'd never stand for what's happening to the land."

"Obviously he has an idea," Amra said, arching an eyebrow at Cavan. "Otherwise he wouldn't make it sound hopeless."

"He *does* do that, doesn't he?" Qalas said, frowning in realization.

"Well, when your skills are limited—" Amra began, but stopped when Cavan cleared his throat.

Amra fluttered her eyelashes with a smile that would have been sweet on anyone else. On Amra, it was pure menace. Playful menace in this case, but still.

Though perhaps Reesa did not yet understand Amra's expressions, because she frowned at the sight. As though she thought Amra might be flirting.

"I do have an idea," Cavan said. "Won't help with everything, but it should at least keep us breathing healthy air."

"Are you up to it?" Ehren asked, in tones of pure practicality.

"Should be. No sign of the spell fire so far. And before you ask, this shouldn't trigger any more of it. It's just that elementals can be a bit … capricious."

"He's hemming and hawing," Qalas said.

Amra sighed. "It means he needs us to behave while he does this, and he's not sure we will."

"There *is* precedent," Cavan said.

"In that instance we were not following the edict of a god," Ehren said, giving Amra a look only he could give: hard eyes, but a small smile. A warning, without pressure.

"Good," Cavan said. "Now this is what I need you to do."

Making arrangements did not take long. Partially because Cavan's friends really were cooperating without complaints or questions — which he could not always count on when it came to his spells — and partially because four of the five horses were well trained enough that persuading the courser to play along was not difficult.

On that front, it helped that Reesa and Horizon had a strong bond.

Soon enough, though, Cavan had everyone arranged the way he wanted them.

The five horses all lay in the gold-and-green wild grass, at the bottom of the hill. Their legs folded underneath them. Their flanks facing inward, and their heads pointing outward, with Dzint facing to the north, then Highsun, Horizon, Caramel, and Ondiq.

Together, the horses' heads formed the points of a star.

Each rider stood by the head of his or her horse, reins in one hand, and a hawk feather in the other.

The tracking torch, Cavan set outside the area he'd paced off. It was unlikely that the simple magics of the tracking torch would affect this casting, but Cavan believed in removing potential variables. So he had planted it in the earth, its violet flame pointing against the oncoming wind.

The wind came from the north, which was good, for that was the direction they had to go. It was also bad, though, because the stench of that wind was foul. That might influence any sylphs that Cavan managed to call in this place.

He could only hope that he could control the spell well enough to call sylphs untainted by the necromancer's magic. Alas, though, the only way to be sure of that would be to ride at least another day's journey south from where they were.

None of them were willing to backtrack that way. Especially not since the necromancer had already moved against them once.

And so, Cavan would have to risk that his control would be sufficient, with a more powerful version of a spell he had cast only a handful of times before.

Not that he would admit any of that aloud.

Facing the north, Cavan held his hawk feather high, and signaled for the others to do the same.

And then, Cavan began the first of the spells he needed to cast. This first prepared the way for what would follow. He chanted words that raised not only the power within himself, but reached out into his surroundings and drew in more power. Power he filtered, taking within the light, nebulous energies of the air, and holding them within himself. Allowing that power to build, build, build.

Once he felt it reaching a peak, he said, "Now."

Cavan reached to the right with his hawk feather, while Ehren reached left. Cavan touched his feather to Ehren's. Ehren then reached right, touching his feather to Reesa's. Reesa repeated the movement to connect her feather with Amra's, and Amra did the same to bridge the connection to Qalas' feather.

Qalas completed the chain by reaching to his right to touch feathers with Cavan.

Power shivered out of Cavan and through the connection into the feathers, which jerked and trembled as though they wished to leap up and fly even without the hawks they'd been attached to.

Cavan and the others all raised their feathers in a single movement.

The way had been prepared. Now came the tricky part.

The chant Cavan began then was not in a language he spoke. Not even with the incomplete command he possessed of the language most of his spells required.

No, this chant was much older. It was said to be old, when even Rentiss was young. That it harkened back to the days when humans first took a stand and demanded space from the elder races, such as the elves, the dwarves and the Dunaians. It was said that the first human wizards of that age forged pacts with the elemental kings, such that any human wizard who called on those pacts could command elemental servants for a time.

Cavan had not cast this spell since it had been proven to him that he carried Dunaian blood. That he was not wholly human. He could not help but wonder if that were the reason these spells had not always worked perfectly for him.

In the moment, though, Cavan had no space for such concerns. He focused on the syllables he had memorized. The rhythms of the chant. And the intentions he held. Even the reasons he needed elemental aid in this instance.

The chant itself took time. It was long, and had to be issued in a single breath, for such were the requirements of the King of Air. And it had to be repeated three hundred seventy-five times, in order to call five elementals with the single spell.

Cavan could only hold up his feather and give himself to his chant. Trust in the skills he had gained, the trials he'd survived since the last time he had called for elementals.

After one hundred repetitions, the wind shifted. Came from the south instead of the north. Cavan could not risk the attention to speculate on what that might mean, or how it might affect his spell.

After the second hundred repetitions, the wind began to swirl about them. Building slowly in strength. This, at least, was expected. Cavan tightened his grip on his feather, and hoped that his friends remembered that this would happen.

Cavan's jaw and tongue were beginning to get sore from giving voice to these awkward syllables, but he kept his focus on his goal and soldiered on.

By the three hundredth repetition, the winds swirled and howled such that Cavan and his friends stood within the eye of a small tornado.

The horses complained, but soothed. Even Cavan's, which meant it was likely Ehren's prayers, not mere horsemanship on the part of Cavan's friends.

At the three hundred and seventy-fifth repetition of that interminable chant, the tornado stopped.

Five sylphs swirled in the air about them. Like tiny, beautiful men and women, with golden yellow skin and long, flowing hair.

"Now!" Cavan cried out, and thrust his feather forward as though stabbing it into an enemy. He cried out the final words of the spell then. The connection between the feathers, the power, the elemental king of air, and that king's five servants.

One of the sylphs, a female, blew Cavan a kiss and slipped inside the feather which had been prepared for her.

Silence followed. Even the wind stilled.

Cavan swallowed. He was drenched in sweat. When had that happened? And how did his throat get so sore?

Oh. Right. That chant.

"Did it work?" Amra asked.

Cavan looked about himself. Where there had been five sylphs flying about, there were none. With his wizard sight he looked at the feathers.

He gave a sigh of relief. Nodded his head.

Ehren thrust a waterskin into Cavan's hand. He drank gratefully. Cool spring water. It tasted like the wonder of the afterlife.

"How will this work?" Qalas asked.

"The feather," Cavan said. "It must stay touching your skin. Tuck it behind your ear if you like, but it would be better tucked close to your heart."

Cavan demonstrated, and the others followed suit.

A breeze trickled down from the north, and Cavan smiled at the immediate difference.

"I'm not..." Amra started, then stopped herself and gave Cavan a grin. "The stench is gone."

"The stench is still there," Ehren corrected her, "even if Cavan's magic has no ensured that it won't trouble us."

"What about the horses?" Amra said. "They don't have feathers."

"While we ride them," Cavan said, "they'll benefit. If we separate, we leave the feathers with the horses."

"Couldn't we have used ten feathers?" Reesa asked.

"Well," Cavan said, trying to hold onto his patience, "I only *have* eight hawk feathers, so two horses would be short anyway. And it doesn't matter. Horses don't have the ... capabilities required to participate in the ritual."

"Can we get moving then?" Qalas asked. "I'd rather get there before midnight. Who knows what that hour does for a necromancer's powers?"

EVEN WITH SYLPHS PURIFYING THE AIR ABOUT CAVAN AND HIS FRIENDS, the ride across that twisted, accursed landscape was not pleasant.

Oh, the *air* was good now. Smelled fresh and clean as it did beside the waterfalls of Holst. But everything else was still ... off.

The ground sounded wrong under the hooves of their horses. It did not squish the way Cavan had dreaded, but their hoofbeats made only a dull sound as they rode.

The suffering of the twisted, yellow-brown grasses and peeling, leafless, yellowed bone trees seemed to cry out to Cavan for aid. For justice. For a priest of the Green Lord to come and cleanse them. To purge them of their struggle and restore to them the breath of life.

Worse, now and again Cavan could see creatures, moving about among the grasses. Things that might have been mice and voles once. But now their eyes glittered red, and their skins hung where they weren't missing. As though they'd been dead for weeks, and refused to simply lie down.

Those were just the prey animals of the area. Cavan worried what the predators would be like...

Amra rode in the lead, holding the tracking torch. Cavan rode just behind her, then Reesa, Ehren, with Qalas watching their rear. Reesa and Qalas rode with their bows in hand. Arrows not nocked, but in ready quivers.

Cavan kept his focus on his wizard sight. Watching mainly for areas of dead but moving grasses, and calling warnings ahead to Amra, so she could steer around them.

Cavan wasn't certain that such low and sickly grasses could offer any threat at all to a cantering horse, even if they were animated by some evil force. But he didn't see the point in risking it.

The terrain here was flat. As though even any hills had died and left behind only the flattened spaces where they'd been.

Cavan and his friends kept to their course now. None of them willing to stop before they had to, even if that meant slowing the horses to a walk, and feeding them during such walks, instead of giving them their proper rest.

So long as they did not push for speed, but settled for a slower devouring of the distance between themselves and their target, the horses were better off this way.

Nothing Cavan nor Ehren could do would make this land a healthy place for the horses to take a proper rest. If worse came to worst, there was a blessing Ehren had used before that would aid the horses stamina. But Cavan was never certain when his friend would deem that blessing appropriate, and when not.

The hours drained past as they rode, and Cavan marked the distance three ways.

First, the progress of the sun through the sky. By now the necromancer would know that a priest of Zatafa rode with them. Sending undead against Ehren while the sun was in the sky, that would only have wasted the necromancer's resources without achieving any useful, tactical goal.

And no necromancer survived to gather this much power — enough to twist the land the way Cavan saw — unless he also had brains.

Second, of course, the tracking torch. Its violet flame flickered taller now than the length of Cavan's hand. And it grew slowly taller yet as they rode.

Finally, and this bit of information Cavan kept to himself for the time being, as the afternoon wore on, he could begin to tell how close they were to the necromancer by wizard sight alone.

Riding with his eyes attuned to the magical side of things, the way he was, Cavan had grown used to the traces of death magic he was seeing, infesting the world about him. He'd begun to ... taste its flavor, which was as close as he could come to explaining it, even to himself.

Irritating, really, that he thought of it as tasting flavor, since most of what he picked up magically came through his vision.

Just another place Cavan's incomplete education failed him, in terms of defining exactly what it was he was doing. How his magical senses really worked.

But the precise descriptors of the process were not necessary to understanding what he observed. And Cavan, he was beginning to develop a stronger and stronger sense of the key identifiers that lay behind the magic of this necromancer.

It was not that Cavan understood that wizard's magical signature, per se. He would have needed to witness more of the necromancer's actual spellwork for that. This was more a deep familiarity that would allow quick recognition in the future.

Cavan could not help comparing it to something he'd learned in warrior training. Ways to recognize people from the way they moved, rather than the features of their faces.

On a battlefield, faces could hide behind helmets. Faces could be hidden by other combatants, or smoke, or any of a hundred other things. But the way someone moved, that was a far easier thing to count on spotting.

Recognizing a magical signature was closer to identifying someone's face. What Cavan was doing as he rode was more like developing a familiarity with the way the necromancer moved, magically speaking.

And that familiarity made it easy for Cavan to realize something. As they rode through the afternoon sunlight, Cavan could begin to see what he thought of as the core of the deathly magical rot he saw in the land all about him.

A core that became more and more obvious as the afternoon wore on. It even felt at times as though they were racing the setting sun, on their way toward that core.

At first, that core was a mere dot on the horizon. So far away, it barely seemed to get closer. Perhaps akin to a distant torch seen across a lonely moor, by night.

But as time passed, eventually, it grew. More like seeing the fire of a distant camp.

Then a closer camp. Cavan found himself glancing at the tracking torch more and more often then. Hoping they were getting close — that the power of this necromancer could only produce a core the size of perhaps a festival bonfire. Though he knew in his gut that they still had some distance to travel.

And the core did not stop at the size of a bonfire.

Past mid-afternoon, the comparison in Cavan's head was akin to a castle whose lights could be seen for some distance.

Then it was as though the castle were lit up for a feast, a blaze that would be seen from towns away.

Then it was as though the castle were lit up for war. Blazing pitch, archers with arrows afire. By then, the sun was setting over the Dwarfmarches, a sight that looked redder and more threating here among this gnarled, abused landscape.

Finally, Cavan could only whistle the halt.

They were here.

8

THE GROUND ALL AROUND CAVAN'S HORSE WAS DEAD. FLAT. PALE. Jagged, with dusty cracks through that claylike smoothness.

No grass here. Not sickened grasses, fighting for life, but at least not the undead grasses either.

Just dry dirt.

The sky above, a spreading purple from the east to the reds and oranges of the setting sun to the west. But here, within the realm of the necromancer, even those normal colors seemed bent. Wrong.

The purples to the east, like bruises. The reds to the west, like those damnable glowing eyes Cavan had been spotting all day on the undead vermin that stalked this land.

The worst of those had been that pack of wolves. Their fur was matted with dried blood, and they each were missing chunks of flesh. And yet they'd still tried to fight with the pack tactics of their living brethren.

They'd never had a chance. Zatafa's glory still rode high in the sky when the wolves had come, and Ehren dispatched them quickly.

But the sight of those eyes, glowing red with hatred for those who still drew breath. That sight would remain with Cavan for some time.

"Why are we stopping?" Amra asked, which almost made Cavan laugh.

Even though she could not have followed the growing sight of the necromancer's center of power, as Cavan had, surely she had to have noticed that the tracking torch's purple flame stood three hands high now, with flares as high as five hands.

Cavan nodded to the torch, then pointed past the grove of dead trees ahead of them.

These trees had once been evergreens of some stripe. Possibly the same type as those Cavan and his friends had camped among only two nights past. Difficult to say, as they looked now.

They had no needles. At all. Not on their branches, nor anywhere among the nearby ground.

Their bark had been stripped, or peeled off, or simply fallen away. Whatever had happened, the bark was gone too. The under-bark that remained was the red of old blood, veined through with streaks of black.

Every limb and twig of those trees remained, but none were lower than twice Cavan's height.

"Through there," Cavan said. "That's where the lair is. We'll need to hobble the horses over here."

"Can you protect them?" Reesa asked, stroking Horizon's nervous brow.

"There are no guarantees, but I can keep most threats away from them," Cavan said, dismounting.

"And Zatafa can aid against threats Cavan cannot manage," Ehren said, swinging down from Highsun's saddle. "But he's right. There are no guarantees."

"Where's the underbrush?" Qalas said, hopping down from Ondiq's saddle, but his eyes all on the trees ahead of them. "Never seen evergreens that didn't have underbrush, but not even skeletons of it remain."

"One thing this necromancer is not," Amra said, "is subtle. Why keep the underbrush, if the twigs will just catch in your robes?"

"Maybe," Cavan said, then he and Ehren gathered the horses

together. Cavan warded them, while Ehren blessed them. And then, it was the time Cavan had begun to dread over the last few hours.

"Feathers," Cavan said. "Tuck them under the saddles, so they won't dislodge accidentally."

Cavan reached into his own shirt, withdrew the feather that held his temporarily bound air elemental, and tucked it safely under Dzint's saddle, while all around him the others did the same.

Gasps and retches all around Cavan. He held his breath and withdrew his touch from the feather.

He tried a breath.

At first, Cavan thought his lungs were failing him. He gasped hard, but didn't seem to draw in air.

By his second breath, he realized he *was* indeed taking in air. But that air had little life to it. Almost like giving seawater to a thirsty man.

Almost. But not quite. The winds of the world still blew, if weakly in this place, and fresh air came into the necromancer's domain to do battle with his deathly influence.

And so while each breath meant far less than it should have, each breath would still contain life enough to sustain them for a time.

Those winds did little to abate the foul taste of each breath though. A decrepit, decayed odor that lingered on the tongue and in the nostrils.

Once Cavan and his friends were as accustomed to this foul air as they were likely to get, they drew their weapons and readied themselves to continue.

Silence. The whisper of the wind, but no buzzing or chirping of insects. No flapping of wings. Not a single sign of the usual activity Cavan would expect while out in the wilderness.

No, he hadn't been expecting any. Steeped in death as this place was, the only sounds Cavan might have heard would have been dead things, coming to kill them.

Still, after hours on horseback and the dull sound of their thudding hooves across this twisted land, the sudden silence disturbed

Cavan. As though the land itself held still, poised and waiting in ambush...

Those trees. Odds were that they were dead, but why risk that the trees weren't *undead*? No. Better to...

Cavan shook his head. First things first.

"Tracking torch," he said, holding out his hand. Amra handed it to him without a word.

Cavan thrust it into the dirt, head down, as he muttered, *"Riwaka."*

The torch extinguished, it's purple light flashing out, and leaving only the fading light of the distant sun.

"Ehren," Cavan said, and Ehren proceeded with the blessing that would allow them to see as though it were bright daylight.

Torches or even the light of a gibbous moon were enough for many nighttime activities. But not here. Not now. Their little group would need every advantage it could get, if they all wanted to live to see the sunrise.

Ehren finished the blessing, and the foul, twisted countryside grew once more as visible as it had been at midday.

Cavan lifted his light, *licha* sword.

"This way," he said, and started to the left around the grove of possibly threatening trees, hoping the blood coloring of their bark was not an omen.

AT LEAST NO UNDERBRUSH MEANT NO TWIGS TO STEP ON OR UNDEAD grasses to grab at Cavan's ankles, as he led his friends around those needleless, blood-red evergreens.

The grove did not look very big. No more than a score and a half of trees, lightly scattered across the span of an arrow's flight. And Cavan could tell that the entrance to the necromancer's lair was on the other side of it. A ruin of some kind.

No reason to pass through those trees. No reason to come close enough, even, for their limbs to reach down and strike at them.

No, Cavan wasn't sure that would happen. But he wasn't going to find out the hard way, either. Not with all the dead things he'd seen moving that day.

But the problem with being surrounded by death magic all day, especially this close to its source, was that much of it began to look and feel the same. Oh, he could have spotted any incoming spells in an instant, but still.

Those trees might have been dead, and they might have been undead. So close to the necromancer's lair, it was difficult to tell without spending precious time on a spell to discern the truth. Easier just to go around them.

Unfortunately, that all-pervasive aura of death magic meant that Cavan had no warning at all when hands reached out of the ground for him.

In that instant, many things happened at once.

Reesa screamed.

Amra's shouted "Ware!" cut through that scream, and her sword cut through something else.

Ehren cried out in Penthix, but the only word Cavan recognized was "Zatafa!"

One set of grayed, but human-looking hands grabbed each of Cavan's ankles and yanked in different directions, as the owners of those hands came up through the ground as though surfacing in a pool.

Falling, Cavan's enchanted blade sliced through one of the forearms, but the hands all still gripped him as his back slammed into the ground.

The fall, Cavan's training kept him ready for. He barked out a breath with his torso tensed for the shock and his head tucked forward so it wouldn't hit. His *licha* armor stole any sting from the short fall.

Both zombies had once been male. But now, even their death shrouds were decayed and falling apart. Though their own grayed skin held together all too well.

A second hack while the zombies found their footing, and Cavan's right leg was free. More or less. Hands still clutched it, but the arms had been severed so his movement of the leg was unimpeded.

From the corner of his eye, in that moment, Cavan could tell how the rest of the fight was going. Each of his friends faced two of these fell zombies.

Amra had evaded being grabbed, and likely cut all four hands free from their owners' arms before her zombies even made it out of the ground. She'd already severed the head and legs from one by then and was swinging at the other.

Ehren's zombies were down on the ground and burning, which explained the even worse odor assailing Cavan's poor nose.

Qalas had evaded one set of hands, and not bothered to sever the other. His first time fighting zombies, perhaps. He'd cut the head from one of his attackers, but all four hands ripped him to the ground.

Reesa was in the worst position. She'd had her bow in hand, and arrows were useless against this kind of zombie. Some could be taken down with arrows through the skull, but the kind with grayish, intact skin had to be hacked apart and burnt.

Her zombies had already dragged her down and one twisted at her legs while the other moved up her body with murderous intent.

Ehren was already moving to help her, so Cavan focused on the two coming after him.

The severed hands crawled their slow way up Cavan's leggings. Their owner moved in swinging its handless arms like clubs. The other, intact zombie continued pulling at Cavan's leg, dragging him on the ground away from his fellows.

Cavan tried kicking the dragging zombie, but that was just reflex. No point in kicking a grayed zombie, unless he could kick hard enough to dislodge a limb. Even Amra couldn't do that.

The handless zombie managed a blow to Cavan's skull then, hard enough that Cavan thought for a moment of the tolling of the Tradeton bell on market day, when he'd been a child living with his foster family.

Cavan sliced right through the knees of the handless zombie. But its momentum led it to fall forward at Cavan. Blows to Cavan's chest then, but his *licha* hauberk stole their strength.

The zombie latched onto the *licha* links with its teeth. Fortunately those teeth would give long before the dune elf steel.

Battle shouts behind Cavan now. Amra and Qalas coordinating, from the sound of it. Plus more of Ehren's prayers.

Unable to reach the dragging zombie with his sword now, and frustrated, Cavan cut through the torso of the handless zombie, but that only made the dragging zombie's load lighter.

The loose hands were still working their way up Cavan's body, likely going for his throat. The handless zombie kept battering at Cavan's chest with its forearms, but Cavan's armor kept him safe from that for now.

He needed to do something about that dragging zombie.

The dragging zombie braced.

Cavan flicked one of the loose hands into the dragging zombie's face.

A moment of distraction, while the dragging zombie cleared away the clutching hand.

All Cavan needed.

With the lighter weight on his chest now, Cavan was able to sit up and slash through the forearms of the dragging zombie.

Not exactly free, but certainly in a better position than he *had* been, Cavan immediately rolled and kicked and struggled to dislodge the remaining hands, as well as the zombie gripping Cavan's armor with its teeth.

Finally, Cavan was free and on his feet. Just in time to see Amra slash through the neck and then waist of Cavan's remaining standing zombie in a graceful, arching swing with her dark sword. Qalas, beside her, bashed open the skull of the biter with the steel-wrapped grip of his halberd's handle.

Ehren strode through then, poking bits of zombie with his staff, while muttering prayers that set those bits to burn so fast and hot they were ash within moments.

"Reesa?" Cavan asked, turning to face her, where she sat, pale and shaking.

She gave Cavan a determined nod, though, and stood.

"My fault," Cavan said, stepping closer while the others disposed of the remaining zombie bits. "We're so used to trusting each other's weapons choice that I didn't think to advise you to switch to your swords, now that we're close."

"Ehren ... already said that," Reesa said, not looking at Cavan while she picked up her bow and slung it over her shoulder. "Verbatim."

"But—"

"Look," Reesa said, turning quickly, her gray eyes blazing. "It was a scare, I admit it. And I'll have some bruises. But I'm all right. And we have work to do."

She drew her short swords.

Cavan gave Reesa and smile and a nod. The smile she returned made her look like Amra's long-lost cousin.

VASTIG WATCHED THE TRAP SPRING FROM HIS HIDDEN PLACE WITHIN THE undead, dried-blood *neelach* trees, just outside the master's lair.

Not a comfortable place — even undead *neelach* trees grumbled objections to his presence — but perfect cover. Even for a banished forest elf. He could dance among these trees and no human would ever see him, so long as he kept his arrows and blades to himself.

And Vastig's goal right now was merely the gathering of information. Yes, he wanted that relic. He craved the feel of it in his hand. But any true hunter knew the importance of learning much about prey before striking.

So Vastig stood where he stood to study this prey.

They possessed enough command of elementals that the air within the necromancer's demesne was only just beginning to trouble them. Worth noting, but not all that impressive.

Further, these humans had been smart enough not to test the

trees. That *might* have been impressive, had they not ridden all day past a great deal of undead vegetation to get to this point.

The one in front. The human whose armor and sword were both dune-elf forged, which only proved the low standards of Vastig's foul cousins from the deserts.

Given what passed for that one's wards around their horses, it seemed likely that this human was the one who considered himself a mighty wizard. And yet he was not even skilled enough to spot the waiting zombies, ready to come for them. Nor did he dispatch any foes with his "arcane might."

Not that this human was any more impressive when it came to playing with his dune elf toys. Knew to dismember grayed zombies, but he still got dragged to the ground, and was on the verge of getting his unprotected head stove in before he finally managed to halt the immediate threat.

As for the others...

The woman with the relic. Oh, how the black, wyrding blade called to Vastig, now that he stood no more than two score steps away. He could feel the song of its dark magics in his bones, his blood...

Vastig shook himself and returned to his observations.

She acquitted herself well enough, Vastig supposed. Likely attributable to the blade's gifts and warnings. She'd leapt free of the grasping hands, and severed her foes with neat, precise strokes.

With that sword in hand, she might even put up a fight, when her time came.

The southerner. With the halberd. Decent reactions, though ignorant of the dangers of grayed zombies. Still, he adjusted to his situation readily enough, and coordinated with the relic-wielder well.

Competent, but he would pose no threat to Vastig.

That priest, though. Up close now, Vastig could see the pristine white of the priest's garments, even after their skirmish. Not to mention the might of his goddess' blessings, through him. Experienced, and firmly in the favor of his goddess.

That priest might pose problems. He was likely the reason those humans had yet to light a torch, though dusk had to be troubling their inferior eyes.

The master would deal with the priest. Vastig would have to be sure the master understood the depth of threat that one might pose.

That left the last one. The woman who fancied herself an archer. She was nothing. Lucky to have been saved by the priest, or she would be dead already.

Oh, now that their brief struggle was over, she drew her swords and brayed sounds of battle, but all humans behaved thus. Or at least, all humans stupid enough to continue on a venture such as this one.

She lacked even the seasoning of her fellows. She had not the intelligence to recognize that she was outmatched and flee. She would fall quickly, when the time came.

But then, at least her flesh was the most likely to be tender. Soft, from an easy life. Marbled, perhaps.

Yes, Vastig would relish most the flesh of the relic-wielder, for it would mean he now held her sword. But of the five of them, the would-be archer, the woman with the hair like honey, she would likely be the tastiest.

Vastig already imagined how each of them would taste. What parts he would eat raw, and how he would prepare the rest.

He got so lost in his mental preparations, that he almost missed the most important sight of the whole scene.

The skirmish was over. The few bruises suffered had been treated with competent herb lore. The humans gathered, they planned, and they moved on.

But the relic-wielder. She kept glancing into the grove of *neelach* trees. Not as though she feared the trees. More as though...

More as though she suspected Vastig's presence.

Oh, what a wondrous idea. Was it too much to hope that Vastig was right?

Some enchanted swords, Vastig knew, could warn of enemies nearby. But only those with currently hostile intent. Often to the point of weapons drawn and readied, such as a waiting ambush.

And yet, here Vastig stood, intending only to watch, and no weapons even in his hands.

Were the relic-wielder of one of the longer-lived races — an elf, or even one of the dwarves or skolach — Vastig might have believed that she had battle-honed instincts warning her of Vastig's possible presence.

But the relic-wielder was a human. And though Vastig was no expert when it came to humans, he believed her to be young in her adulthood. Certainly she lacked the wrinkles and hair colors that indicated what humans considered old age.

She could not have the instincts or experience necessary to suspect Vastig's presence. To look over once to check for a possible observer, that was not beyond the bounds of reason, even for one such as her. But to continue looking? Even though her senses gave no confirmation of a *reason* to keep checking?

No. No youthful human woman could have such finely honed battle instincts.

That meant the sword had to be warning her. Perhaps the sword even knew of Vastig's precise location, but the relic-wielder was too arrogant to listen or too dull to hear.

Either way, first the relic saved her life from an arrow she could never have seen coming. Then it warned her of the zombies from below. Now it even seemed to be warning her about Vastig.

Truly, a masterwork of some ancient, arcane smith. Perhaps even Dunaian.

Oh, when the blade at last found itself in Vastig's hands. Then, *then* would both blade and wielder meet their equal.

Vastig could almost see his enemies falling before him, one by one by one. Names he'd not spoken in decades trembled near his lips to be bellowed as he struck...

Soon.

NIGHT WAS FALLING, EVEN IF ZATAFA'S BLESSING KEPT IT LOOKING LIKE day to Cavan's eyes. The foul, half-dead air grew chill.

No buzz of insects. No padding feet of forest creatures. The ground around here was so dead that not even undead grasses remained. Just that oddly smooth clay that seemed to muffle even their footsteps.

The only sounds Cavan heard were those made by himself and his friends, as they made their cautious way forward.

His stomach growled a small complaint. The lunch they'd shared while riding — strips of beef and cheese, along with a pungent, sour-sweet blue fruit called dalas — had been hours ago.

Not that Cavan's mouth could consider the possibility of food. Not here, rounding the end of that grove of those disturbing and hopefully dead trees.

Past the grove lay a ruin. The frame of gray stone walls remained, indicating a pentagonal shape to the building that once stood there, though none of those fallen walls stood even as high as Cavan's collar now.

The building had once been the size of an inn, by Cavan's estimate. With the remains of a smaller, wooden outbuilding now a crumbled wreck to one side.

"It was a monastery," Ehren said, his voice reverent.

"How can you tell?" Cavan asked.

"The shape, for one," Ehren said. "Five-sided building, consistent with the Order of Blessed Light. Note the small stars engraved along the bottom edge of the stonework. Another indicator."

"The star followers?" Reesa asked, using the common name for the Order of Blessed Light. "Those stories were real?"

"What stories?" Cavan asked, while Amra huffed out an impatient breath.

"Stories they told us as children. Scary, harvest festival stuff. Seems that—"

"Excuse me," Amra said, with far more patience than she would have shown for Cavan, or anyone else for that matter. "But do any of those stories involve a necromancer?"

"No," Reesa said slowly, frowning. "Not the ones I heard."

"Then they'll keep."

"Roof's gone," Qalas said, gesturing to the ground with his halberd. "Completely. The remains of that wooden outbuilding are still here, but the roof of the main building is gone. So are any shutters they had."

"Just like the undergrowth," Cavan said.

"Hold here," Amra said. In three swift movements across fallen chunks of monastery she stood atop the nearest section of wall, her sword still naked in her hands.

"I see a likely entrance," she said, then jumped back down to the ground with the grace and silence of a forest cat. "Toward the back of the stone floor. Wooden trap door, likely a staircase leading down to the old cellar, and whatever else is down there now."

"Trap being the operative word," Cavan said, and Amra nodded.

"Why?" Reesa asked.

"One," Cavan said, "it's too easy and too obvious an entrance. Two, it's the only wood left in that building. We could check it out, but even getting close is likely to trigger the trap."

"So do we hit it now or later?" Qalas asked, which got him a look of disbelief from Amra.

"What?" he asked. "You want to leave it here for future travelers to trip?"

"Later," Cavan said. "If we survive this, we'll clear the trap by daylight. If not," — Cavan looked around — "one more hazard won't make a difference in this place."

Qalas frowned, but nodded.

Amra turned an expectant look on Cavan. He smirked and sheathed his sword.

"Get ready," Cavan said, rubbing his hands together. "This is going to go one of two ways. If the necromancer wants us to come in and fight on his terms, I'll find the real entrance no problem. If the necromancer wants to keep us out, just trying to find the entrance by magic will get some kind of guards after us."

"Can't we find it without magic then?" Reesa asked.

"That's the problem when dealing with magic," Qalas said while

Amra just shook her head. "If you know how close someone has to be to *find* your secret entrance without magical aid, then you just set your enchanted safeguards a little bit farther out."

"At least wizards hardly ever bother with non-magical approaches," Amra said, and it was Qalas' turn to nod.

"Couldn't Zatafa—" Reesa began, but Ehren interrupted her. Gently.

"Alas," he said, though his lips still held a small smile, "even Zatafa is not all powerful. Which is really as it ought to be. If the gods did not leave us space to deal with our own problems—"

"Ehren," Amra said, fluttering her eyelashes, "is this the right time for a lecture?"

"It's hardly a lecture."

Cavan cleared his throat.

Qalas snorted and said to Reesa, "In case you're wondering, yes. They're always like this."

Reesa's frown looked more puzzled than disapproving. And her eyes darted back and forth, as though Amra, Ehren and Qalas weren't casually positioning themselves to watch every direction while Cavan prepared to cast a spell.

Cavan ushered his friends back a few steps, then turned to begin what he needed to do.

Cavan had kept his wizard eyes open most of the day, and truth was, that had given him a small headache. He could ignore it, set it aside, without too much trouble. But for what he was about to do, he needed to acknowledge his current state.

And that state included a headache. Although some of that might have just been the effect of staring at death everywhere he looked.

Of course, that ride had been gentle, compared to what surrounded him now. This ruined monastery practically seethed with necromancy.

But Cavan could not seek any relief yet. Worse, he needed to get more precise about what he saw. Dig through all the ambient necro-mantic spellwork and find any active or readied spells.

He began by emphasizing his sight in the most basic way. A repetition and reinforcement of his usual detection methods.

He covered his eyes with his palms. Whispered.

"Neela asa. A ta asa neelasa."

When Cavan opened his eyes, his stomach clenched, and he was glad he hadn't eaten recently. So very much fell magic here. Steeped into the stones of the ruined monastery. Far too much for a single necromancer to have accomplished, unless he'd been ensconced here for centuries.

More than that, Cavan could tell not only that many of the lingering effects were *not* necromancy — at least some involved demons, and other dark magics — but he was certain that much of what he saw came from other, unknown evil wizards.

Cavan had spent the day learning the way this necromancer moved, magically speaking. And the metaphorical movements Cavan could see now, flowing out of the ground and around the very stones of the fallen monastery, suggested at least a dozen different spell-casters.

Good. That much was good, at least. Cavan could focus down on the one style and approach — the movement, as it were — he needed to follow.

"Can see why he chose this place," Cavan muttered, though in the silence surrounding him his words were doubtless heard by all his companions. "Been a source of foul magics for a long, long time."

Reesa started to say something, but the others hushed her.

Cavan swept his line of sight across the whole area surrounding the monastery, from where he stood to as far forward as he could see.

Too difficult to be sure. There had just been too much magic here for anything like the simple approach to help.

Then again, Cavan had determined one thing already. He'd cast a spell close to the monastery, and yet not gotten a response. That likely meant that the other spells he considered would not trigger a response either.

Which meant the necromancer *did* want them to enter his lair, where he would hold all the advantages.

Wonderful.

At least it was enough information for Cavan to proceed.

One deep breath would normally have been all Cavan needed to clear his thoughts and double his focus on what he was doing. In this place, however, he needed three breaths to get enough good air for the same effect.

But one thing Cavan had learned over the years was the art of improvisation. And so he turned the three breaths into a triple-breath, using the physicality of the movements to deepen his mind further than a good, single breath would have done on its own.

Mind games, true, but it seemed to Cavan sometimes that the deeper mysteries of magic all involved mind games that wizards played with themselves.

The spell Cavan cast then was one of his own invention. Stitched together through experience and innovation from bits of other spells.

From the enhancement of wizard sight, he pulled in aspects of increased sensitivity.

From the elements of basic warding, he pulled in aspects that detected magical threats, as well as things hidden through illusions.

From the elements of basic enchantment, he worked with the keys of magic tied to physical objects.

The next part of this spell, Cavan would have had trouble explaining to another wizard. The concept of spell structure and technique as the equivalent of movement. Cavan lacked the necromancer's signature, which would have made this spell much easier, but by trusting his gut he could tweak his nouns to follow spells designed around the necromancer's metaphorical way of moving.

And finally, he combined all these parts of spells together with something he'd worked out during his short-lived attempt at life as a thief. (Cavan had just never been able to bring himself to rob someone who didn't really, *really* deserve it.) A means of finding entrances — as well as cubbies, alcoves, safes and the like — that were concealed by ordinary means.

Cavan pulled a stub of dirty, white candle from his spell pouch. No longer or broader than the first joint of his thumb, with a small, blackened wick, and tiny runes etched into the sides. From other pockets in that pouch, he pulled out the right combination of herbs and ground them into the wick with his fingers.

He breathed power across the wick as he whispered, *"Ne maja haka asa, kol no ari tassa fela."*

To Cavan's eyes, the wick flared to life. A small, white flame, that no one else would be able to see.

"Follow me," Cavan said to the others without looking back, "and be ready."

Cavan held the candle up ahead of himself, and the flame tipped to the right. Cavan turned with it and followed.

At first it looked to be leading Cavan to the right side of the ruined monastery, but no. The wick sputtered a moment, through reds and blues, before returning to white, and leaning farther to the right.

Just as Cavan had suspected. The crumbled remains of the outbuilding.

Sure enough, the candle flame led him there. It cycled through yellows and reds, and finally flashed black then white, over and over.

The yellows and reds, like most of those other colors, had only been signs of other, older, lingering magics. Things that a wizard of properly evil bent could probably tap into and resuscitate, a thought that made Cavan shudder involuntarily.

The black though, that was the color of necromancy to this spell. More evidence that the necromancer himself came and went through the entrance concealed here.

The white indicated that there was nothing here that could present an immediate danger. No trap waiting to drain the life of anyone without the proper passcode, for example.

Oh, there was a small ward. Cavan could see that without the candle. A simple thing, mostly intended to alert the necromancer if anyone entered. But nothing more dangerous was waiting here.

Cavan snorted. The only ward would be easy enough to defeat.

One of the problems of necromancy, after all. It was an ... invasive art, and decayed the necromancer's ability to cast spells that did not require a touch of death.

And from what Cavan had been riding through all day, he felt certain this necromancer was only capable of two kinds of wards: the most basic wards, and the most lethal.

These were the most basic.

Cavan extinguished his spell candle and reached out with a flare of power toward the weakest spot in the ward. It died without a struggle.

"We're good," Cavan said, putting away the candle and drawing his sword once more. Knowing exactly where the entrance was now, Cavan could see the pattern hidden within the ancient, rotted debris.

He tapped it. Amra nodded.

Holding her sword in one hand now, she reached with her other fingers for purchase and swung open the concealed trapdoor.

A series of solid, stone steps led the way down. That was the good news.

The bad news was that Cavan's luck continued to follow its current trend — bad. He could hear a series of alarm gongs ringing somewhere down those stairs.

Amra shot a quick grin at Cavan.

"Didn't think to check for nonmagical triggers, did you?"

Cavan shook his head.

"Of course," Qalas groaned. "Of course this is the *one* wizard who uses nonmagical alerts."

"Good," Amra said, turning to the staircase. "Wouldn't want this to be *too* easy."

Frankly, Cavan wouldn't have minded something easy, for a change. No point in expressing that, though. Amra wasn't going to stop for wit.

She led the way down into the necromancer's lair.

VASTIG WAITED UNTIL HE HEARD THE SOUNDS OF BATTLE BEFORE HE left his hiding spot along the edge of the blood red *neelach* trees, near the ruined monastery and crept forward along the muted ground.

His first assessment of this group had been wrong. Exciting, in how infrequently that happened. Boring, in that it did not seem to make this group the more dangerous.

Back at the Forest of Risen Knights, Vastig had gathered that a group of three were escorting two wealthy humans, likely a young couple running away from their parents.

Instead, it was clear by now that four of these humans were accustomed to traveling together, although one of their number had only joined them relatively recently. The southerner with the halberd. He had not yet meshed as tightly as the priest, the relic-wielder, and the would-be wizard.

The would-be archer was the puzzle. Why would the others bring her along? She was unused to their life of travel, and from what Vastig had seen of her only fight, she had little to offer.

It was possible she'd hired the four of them as an escort, but that would not explain why she'd let them leave their travel route for a fool's errand such as this one.

No, she was not their leader nor their employer.

Perhaps she was skilled at pleasure? Humans seemed to value that above...

No. That did not seem likely. None of them had smelled of recent sex before they'd entered the hidden stairway. If they'd brought her along for that purpose, surely *one* of them would have indulged last night.

Perhaps Vastig would ask her purpose of one of them, before delivering a final blow. The answer could prove useful, the next time Vastig hunted humans.

A moment of silence. Vastig paused perhaps three steps from the open hidden entrance.

No sound of rapid footfalls. No cries of panic. No wails for the dead. Nothing more than, perhaps, hushed conversation. In the silence of this place, Vastig's ears could not discern the details.

Nevertheless. Likely then that the five humans had all survived their struggle against the first wave of grayed zombies called forth when they tripped the alarm gongs.

Vastig smiled. The nonmagical alarm had been his idea. It would call forth three waves of grayed zombies, with one wave of blackened zombies in between. The master had approved of its deviousness.

The humans would have a rhythm down by then, from fighting the first two waves of grayed zombies. They'd be expecting that fire would quickly dispatch their foes.

Blackened zombies, of course, were immune to fire.

The final wave of grayed zombies would strike before the last blackened zombie fell.

Oh, for humans, the four primaries of this group seemed competent enough. Especially with that priest to aid them. And, of course, the relic.

The would-be archer might die somewhere in their struggle against the waves of zombies, but the others would survive.

Still, the fights would tax them. Soften them, before they reached the first real threat.

What would that be?

The master refused to waste his magic on more traps, no matter how Vastig pleaded their effectiveness. And it had been so long since any would-be hero had invaded that likely, the master would be worried.

The reeves, he would keep close to him, for his own safety.

No. The master would send Doris.

Perfect.

Doris might terrify them into fleeing, which would make them easy targets for Vastig's arrows. Or else, they would fight her, and perhaps Vastig would find a key moment to finish off the relic-wielder, and then the others would fall easily.

Vastig could practically taste his vengeance, sweet and savory combined on his tongue.

He took his first silent steps down the hidden staircase. Slowly. Oh, so slowly.

9

Cavan's only consolation was that he wasn't the only one breathing hard. Qalas had one hand on his knee, though his other still held his halberd good and ready. Ehren leaned on his staff, and his nose flared wide and often as he tried to gain a reasonable amount of actual benefit from the half-dead air down here.

The priest still looked as though he'd just bathed and donned clothes fresh from the laundress, but at least he was showing *some* signs of effort.

Reesa, of course, was panting and sweaty and leaning back against a wall, but she wasn't as used to things like this as the rest of them. She'd acquitted herself well enough against the grayed zombies, though, and she even did fairly well against the blackened zombies, thinking to sever one's head with a double-stroke of her short swords.

Amra, of course, seemed as tireless as ever. If the state of the air down here even affected her, Cavan couldn't tell.

Some things in this life were just not fair.

At least she was a bit banged up, and as covered in zombie detritus as the rest of them, save Ehren,

Even now, Amra was standing rear guard, certain that they were being followed. Not that Cavan could see or hear any sign of such a thing.

At least they had this moment to catch what breath they could, in this foul place, while Ehren passed out blessed oranges, to cope with the bruises — and a couple of bites — suffered from the attacks, as well as help them regain vibrancy that the air down here tried to steal.

And it was no wonder all of them needed oranges. Four total waves of zombies. Nearly sixty in all. And they'd had plenty of room to swarm as they'd come.

To judge by this place, the old monks must have lived mostly underground. And though space above looked to be at a premium, down here they were downright extravagant with it.

One main hall had led from the bottom of the stairs. Stone and mortar, all around. Wide enough that Cavan and his friends could have brought their horses and ridden, if they'd been willing to risk their horses in the lair of a necromancer.

Well, not quite tall enough for that ride. Almost as though the monks didn't want mounted soldiers swinging swords while riding through their basement.

Cavan couldn't help feeling a flash of curiosity about whether or not that had been a consideration.

The hall had led back toward the monastery, at first, but then it had bent sharply to the right, and continued. Each bend after that had brought with it a wave of zombies.

Sconces for torches every so often, but so full of dust and cobwebs, it didn't seem likely that any torches had been lit down here in hundreds of years.

The floors were not quite so dusty, though they did smell of must and age. Clearly the necromancer, or at least some of his minions, came and went through here regularly.

There had been a few passages or rooms off of this main hall, but they'd been long since walled up. Cavan had checked those areas by both magical and nonmagical methods, but they were not concealing passages or doors.

That did leave the question of where some of those zombies had come from. The ones that had attacked from the rear. Amra's theory was that they dropped from the ceiling, and Cavan saw no reason to dispute it. Troubling idea though.

"Ready?" Amra asked, her voice hushed and her eyes still watching their rear. After the chorus of assent, she spoke to Qalas, voice barely loud enough for Cavan to hear.

"Take point a while. I think that forest elf is behind us again."

"Think we should bring the fight to him?" Qalas asked, just as quiet.

"No," Amra said, frowning. "Too much advantage. He knows this place." She glanced around at the hall. "Besides, there's precious little cover. I don't relish charging a forest elf with a bow in this place. Not if I don't have to."

"If we let him pick his timing..." Cavan said, letting the rest of the sentence finish itself.

"I know," Amra said. "But right now he's out of range. I figure he'll take his chance when we're *not* being hit from all sides."

"I could call up a mist—"

A green mist seeped around them now, but it wasn't a mist called forth by Cavan. And it wasn't immediately dangerous, Cavan could tell that as well. Though the origin of the mist was no doubt magical, it seemed to offer no risk of harm.

Which was good, because Cavan had been worried that the necromancer would have spells that could just seep among them and drain their lives away. Not because Cavan had ever read that necromancers possessed such powers in any book of wizardry, but because he, too, enjoyed the stories of bards.

At least, he enjoyed them in taverns and around fires. At the moment, he would rather not recall such things.

Cavan turned to assure the others that this green mist was not an immediate threat—

—and realized he stood alone in the hallway.

The *dim* hallway. Not full dark, as it would be without Ehren's blessing, but nevertheless not as bright as it ought to be. Was that because he was separated from Ehren?

Cavan gripped the hilt of his sword, and dipped fingers into his pouch of spells.

Someone clucked their tongue, and the echo of that sound seemed to slither around Cavan.

"Such a waste of a pretty, pretty boy. No, no, no, pretty boy. Do not draw your weapons. Your spells. Do not die without need."

No speaker to go with the voice, but the voice was female. Would have sounded like a pleasant singing voice, if not for a rough undercurrent to it. As though the speaker enjoyed inflicting pain.

Well, also the fact that the voice seemed to be coming from everywhere at once added to the creepy factor.

Footsteps then, coming from ahead. But not the slow, measured footstep of a menacing figure, but the rushed, hurried footfalls of someone running in a panic.

Around the next bend in the hall came...

...a girl? Redheaded and young and lovely, even pale with fear and running for her life. She wore a torn, blue linen dress, and she'd lost one of her shoes.

Wait.

Cavan recognized her.

Riverbend, wasn't it? The serving girl who had arrived for their assignation to find Cavan stark naked from his bath and sitting in a pool of blood on the floor, having just defeated two would-be assassins.

She'd run screaming then, too, but *away* from Cavan. Not that he blamed her. What was her name...

"Polli?" Cavan said, slack-jawed in shock to find her here and now.

"Cavan!" Polli cried and ran to him. Clutched him as though she could hide inside him from whatever followed her.

That voice was laughing. "Silly girl, pretty girl, thinks she can get away. No, no, no. No escape for you, pretty girl. Silly girl. Doris always finds her playmates."

Cavan could hear it approaching now. A slithering, thumping sort of gait.

Cavan slipped one consoling arm around Polli, keeping his sword arm free.

"Don't let her get me, Cavan," Polli said. "She has the face of a woman, but *the rest of her*."

Polli shuddered.

"Catch you both," the voice said, still somehow coming from all around Cavan. "Pretty, pretty, pretty. Then we play. Then we eat. Pretty tastes best."

Cavan could see the shadow of this thing now, just around the corner. The shadow looked to have a head at the end of a serpentine neck, followed by a great bulk of...

Wait. *Shadow?*

With Ehren's blessing still at least somewhat in effect?

Cavan tried to shove Polli away, but too late.

Polli latched onto Cavan's throat like a lamprey, dozens of tiny teeth ripping his flesh while she sucked in as though trying to inhale him all at once.

Pain flared through every nerve in Cavan's body. As though acid came in through the place "Polli" bit him and spread swiftly through his veins and arteries.

Reflexes demanded that he stab her with his magic sword. But Cavan's muscles refused to listen to his wise reflexes. Something about the nature of the creature's bite.

Cavan screamed. It was all his muscles would do.

Fortunately, the last-ditch defense he'd set up weeks back came to the fore now, when he needed it most.

The ruby at the bottom of the hilt of Cavan's sword was as fine a gem as any Cavan had ever seen, and he'd been raised by the best jeweler in Oltoss.

A ruby tuned so fine it could hold a few ready spells.

Cavan had cast into that ruby only a handful of spells, most of which would allow him to cast his most important combat spells if he found himself without access to his spell pouch.

However, there was one spell in that ruby that Cavan kept ready for emergencies. Such as an undead creature sucking out his life's blood while he could do nothing, physically, about it but scream.

Cavan's scream of distress and pain triggered the spell.

His sword leapt to attack without Cavan's muscles having any say in the matter. Stabbed right through the heart of the thing wearing Polli's face.

"Polli" detached long enough to cry out in pain. But Cavan's spell wasn't finished.

It was busy unleashing the most powerful weapon Cavan could bring to bear on any enemy: primal fire. Flame called forth from the essential nature of the element itself.

The last time Cavan had used a spell that brought forth primal fire, he, Amra and Ehren had been traveling along the borderlands between this world and the Underworld, and facing a monstrous spider.

Cavan had lost control of the spell then, destroying not only the spider that threatened them, but others, as well as a great deal of the forest in the area. Possibly the whole of that huge forest.

But with a *licha* blade to act as a limiting factor, the primal fire flared out so blue it edged on ultraviolet, no more than a hand's breadth outward from the dune elf steel.

More than enough to do its job.

"Polli" didn't have time to scream again. She burnt to ash, and Cavan tumbled to the ground.

CAVAN LAY ON THE HARD STONE OF THE HALLWAY FLOOR, HIS BLADE still clutched in his white-knuckled hand, though his spell had run its course and the primal fire was gone.

Ehren knelt over him, slathering some kind of sticky, orange paste over Cavan's wounded throat, while murmuring prayers. The paste smelled like swamp muck, but its cool relief was welcome enough.

Of the five of them, only Ehren and Amra had been unharmed by the attack of … whatever that thing had been.

Qalas had seen his sister. Believed the sight, because she was every bit as "headstrong and prone to violence" as he was, and might well have traveled this direction since he'd last seen her.

Amra had seen a champion she had defeated down in Dunlap once, but the fight had been so good the two of them had spent the next week in bed together.

She hadn't been taken in for a moment.

"If Rol had been weak enough to run blubbering up to me like I was his mother, he'd never have given me a fight in the first place."

Ehren hadn't named the woman he'd seen, but he had sounded just as certain that she would never be found here in the lair of a necromancer. Not that it mattered. The moment the hall had dimmed, Ehren had spotted it for an illusion, and kept the thing at bay with his staff.

Reesa had seen Cavan, wounded and desperate for help, which Cavan knew he'd hear about from Amra for months to follow.

In the moment, Amra had contented herself to smirk and say, "Very believable."

When Cavan's turn to talk had come, he didn't name whom he'd seen. But that he hadn't seen Reesa would give him something to think about, when he could afford the luxury of such thoughts.

Qalas had suffered a decent bite, as Cavan had, but Reesa had come out the worst. Even now, she was pale, and having trouble devouring one of Ehren's blessed oranges.

Ehren didn't offer oranges to Qalas or Cavan. He had too few to risk more of them just yet. Especially since there might yet be worse need ahead of them. The smelly pastes would have to suffice, though they left Cavan's neck and jaw feeling stiff and sore.

Not even time for a poultice. Everyone felt sure the next attack was coming soon.

Still, better stiff and smelling of river muck than feeling more acid through his veins while his life's blood drained away.

"So how did we beat it?" Qalas asked, watching the front.

"Never got within striking distance of me," Amra said.

"Me either," Ehren said, and he grimaced as he continued, "and my prayers seemed to amuse it."

"Tell you later," Cavan said. "Let's push on."

Cavan took the lead then, with Qalas behind him, then Ehren and Reesa side by side, and Amra still watching the rear for the elvish archer.

The next bend in the hall wasn't really a bend. It was a room. A junction point of some sort, by the look of it. The ceiling in here arched about the height of a good silver maple tree, and Cavan would have needed three dozen running strides to cross it.

Five other passages led out from here. A line of granite just above those passages circled the room, with symbols every few paces that had been chipped away so badly there was no telling what they were originally.

More wall sconces for torches that hadn't been used in ages. And alcoves along the walls appeared to have been walled off, like the other passages and doorways back down the hallway behind Cavan.

The star of the Order of Blessed Light remained engraved on the floor, large enough that its points touched the circular walls in between, leaving only a sixth section of wall untouched by the star.

"Just what do these monks do?" Qalas asked, frowning.

The ground shook with the thunder of hooves.

"I'm betting they don't ride horses," Cavan said, "but—"

Amra shouted over the rest of his joke.

"Back down the hallway. Now!"

Amra led the way, leaving Cavan the last out of the huge chamber, just as the knights arrived.

And they were definitely the knights whose spirits Cavan had seen back where the messenger from Istanlos appeared to them. Cavan recognized the armor here, and the coat of arms there.

All dozen of those men and women, still ahorse, with longswords, maces and flails in their hands.

Cavan began to wonder what happened to the raiders, but then the chill hit him.

The chill of the grave seemed to seep outward from the knights. An involuntary shiver ran through Cavan and his friends. It was an unnatural cold, and Cavan immediately worried about what effects it would have that he could not predict.

In the immediate, his joints stiffened up, and the wound on his throat ached.

The knights formed ranks. One in the lead, then two-by-two, with one more riding rear guard.

They charged toward the hall where Cavan and his friends pressed themselves against the walls, to avoid getting trampled. Cavan, Reesa and Amra on one side, Qalas and Ehren on the other.

Closer the knights came, building speed.

Cavan readied his sword. His limbs moved slower than they should have, but he felt confident he could cut down the legs of that first horse with his *licha* blade, which should spoil the charge.

Closer still they came. The roar of their hooves echoed from the stone walls and ceiling.

The unnatural chill doubled in strength. Cavan's arms cramped, as did his legs. From hisses of breath down the hall from him, he suspected he was not alone in this.

Cavan could see the milky white of the lead knight's eyes now. His brows were heavy and down, his beard still full and red, and his dead skin only a touch sallow. He controlled his horse with his knees, using both hands to ready his great sword.

Cavan checked his grip.

Just then Qalas cried out, in Rentakat, the language of his home-land, Rentaka.

Rentakat was one of the few human languages not derived from ancient Rentissi, and Cavan spoke little of the tongue himself. But if he heard right, Qalas said:

"Istanlos, by Your will we have ridden hard and found the defiled remains. By the blood of the Godkiller I beg You. Drain the curse from these pour souls, that we may face the" — doer? Perpetrator? Yes, that made more sense — *"perpetrator of this anathema."*

And to Cavan's surprise, Istanlos heard Qalas' plea.

As one, the knights and their steeds all fell. The spells that held them together melted away, leaving only bones and rusted armor and weapons, all of which scattered down the hallway, carried by their momentum.

That bone-chill to the air evaporated as though it had never existed.

For a moment, the only sound was the scattering of bone and metal.

But then the star in the junction room flared to life, a sickly, bloody red glow that gave off a kind of moist heat.

Standing within that star was the necromancer. And he wasn't alone.

———

Cavan was grateful for one thing. That glowing red star engraved into the stonework of the floor had the five sides of the Order of the Blessed Light, and not the seven sides that the necromancer could have used for the worst sorts of spells.

But in the moment, Cavan didn't feel much else to be grateful for.

When Cavan had seen the image of this necromancer in his spell of hindsight, the evil wizard had not looked very impressive. Middling height. Hazel eyes. Wrinkled, ruddy skin, and white, fluffy hair surrounding the tonsure on his scalp.

But here, the purple and dark blue symbols woven into his black robes glowed enough to be seen over the reddish light of the star.

The old, carved thigh bone that the necromancer held aloft, his wand, had more symbols that glowed in harmony with the ones on that robe.

The hindsight spell had not prepared Cavan for the necromancer's aura of power. Stronger than any he'd seen since Master Powys. Strong enough to beat at his senses without a hint of effort, even where Cavan stood.

And standing ready at the necromancer's back, another force of creatures called from the grave.

These ... well, Cavan wasn't sure what they'd been in life. If they'd ever truly been alive. That was a question Cavan did not know about ghouls, and he was looking at ghouls right now. At least two dozen of them.

Their arms and legs were too long for their torsos. Torsos that were thin, save for their bloated bellies. Their skin looked scabrous and bruised all over. What hair they had lay matted and greasy against their scalps.

But their hands and feet ended in talons instead of nails. And their wide mouths, all too full of long, pointed, yellowed teeth.

Their mere presence filled the air with the smell of grave dirt and old blood. And they made a constant, hushed gibbering sound.

The necromancer spoke first.

"Kill them all," he called in a disturbingly high, clear voice, "starting with the priest!"

The ghouls poured forward in a wave.

Cavan charged forward as though taking the fight to the ghouls. He scattered bits of shaved carrot on the stones and cried out, *"Hyasi!"*

He sprang high into the air while the ghouls ran past below him, too focused on getting at Ehren to worry about Cavan. Cavan could only hope Ehren and the others were ready for them.

Cavan's focus was on the necromancer, who watched with an amused eye. He lifted his wand as Cavan came down, but Cavan was ready.

He tossed sand into the air and sucked in as he breathed the words, *"Ulta na-sach."*

Silence purer than anything Cavan had ridden through that day. No scrabbling and gibbering of ghouls. No sounds of battle behind him.

Most important, whatever incantation the necromancer cried out failed.

Cavan brought the momentum of his leap to bear as he swung his sword at the necromancer, aiming for the throat.

The necromancer parried with his wand.

It seemed unfair somehow. Cavan's sword could cleave through many things, could even shear shards from lesser swords. True, there were staves he'd heard of that might have stood against his blade, but a wand?

And yet, that wand parried the blow as though it had been a *licha* sword itself. And worse, the bone wand did not so much as budge an inch under the force of Cavan's assault. As though it had sucked the momentum from...

No. Not sucked. Killed. Of course. Had to be death magic.

The necromancer looked furious, as Cavan landed gently on the stones. Even managed a grim smile as he parried two more of Cavan's rapid sword strokes.

Spry, for such an old man. Had to have stolen the vitality from many.

Just then, the purple symbols on the necromancer's robe and wand flared bright, and Cavan could hear gibbering, slobbering and pounding somewhere behind him, as well as...

...the ring of steel? Did one of the ghouls carry a weapon?

"Better than I expected," the necromancer said, as he continued to parry more of Cavan's attacks. "Properly dealt with, you'll be worthy to add to my resources. Perhaps even worth the cost of my vargamort."

"Is that what that was?" Cavan asked, drawing his spelled dagger with his off-hand. This dagger was thin, twin-edged, with a wooden handle molded to Cavan's grip. Runes etched into the blade carried a spell he had prepared himself.

"Fool," the necromancer said, and spat a word that slipped away from Cavan's mind, even as he heard it.

But the word shunted power through the wand. Power that arced across the tight space between them, slipped around Cavan's spelled dagger to strike.

Pain. Like claws raking down Cavan's very soul. The world seemed to tunnel down on him. Cavan fought to keep his focus on his foe, where it needed to be.

Not foe. Foes.

It seemed as though there were two of the necromancer now. And both of them wielded that wand like a sword on the attack.

Cavan felt hard pressed to keep that wand from touching him, needing both his sword and his dagger to maintain his defense.

He wasn't sure what would happen if the wand touched him, but finding out sounded like a very, very bad idea.

Both Cavan's hands were busy, just keeping that enchanted thigh bone at bay. So how could he strike back?

Spells. He must have known a spell or two that could help here. But whatever that ripping sensation through his core had been, it seemed to have cut him off from his magic.

Cavan could not think of a single spell. Not one. His mind reached for where they should have been, but could not grasp them.

The necromancer began pressing Cavan backward.

***

"KILL THEM ALL, STARTING WITH THE PRIEST!"

Just the order Vastig had hoped for. Those ghouls would focus on the priest. The priest's friends would come to his aid. And Vastig could deal with the relic-wielder on his own.

His bow was ready. His arrow nocked.

She whirled, frowning, sword raised and ready to parry. No doubt the relic warned her of danger for the last time...

No.

This was not the proper way for him to claim a relic. To shoot the current wielder with a bow was to imply he feared to face her. The relic might sense that. Reject him as a wielder.

Intolerable.

Besides, for however powerful the relic might make her, she was still a human, and youthful. She could not possibly be a match for Vastig.

Instead he smiled at her frown. Tossed aside his bow.

Silence?

The bow should have clattered on the ground. Vastig's ears should have heard his lips issue the traditional cry of challenge as he drew his swords. His throat certainly vibrated correctly.

But silence had fallen. What was that fool necromancer playing at?

Nevertheless, Vastig ran at the relic-wielder. And fool that she was, she smiled and ran to meet him.

Suddenly a blindingly golden dome sprang into being farther down the hall. The priest's work, most likely. The ghouls might have trouble with it, but the necromancer would bring it down soon enough.

For now, Vastig had a fight on his hands.

Still, the glare of that dome made him wince. Stop running, even as the relic-wielder closed. Stole the first blow from him.

The first strike should have been Vastig's. He'd imagined it for days. A feint low with his left sword, and a high right strike with the other.

Instead, the relic-wielder, grinning with undeserved courage, came in high as though to part Vastig's head from his shoulders in a single strike.

Vastig's head, of course, was not there when the blow came. Still, between the glare and the ferocity of the strike, Vastig had been unable to properly counter. The most he could do was parry the next attack, this one lower. Toward his waist.

Vastig's arm jarred from the impact of the blow. Sparks flew, and a notch had been taken from one of his blades.

Soon enough, that would not matter.

First, though, he had to regain the advantage. Right now, this grinning woman battered at Vastig's defenses, driving him backward. Attacking with such speed that Vastig had to keep both swords whirling in parries that dug more notches from his blades.

Sound returned to the world.

"Should have kept the bow," the relic-wielder taunted. "Might have had a chance."

"You are nothing without that sword," Vastig said, managing his first counter strike. A weak stab with his lesser hand. All too easy for her to evade. But it was a beginning.

"Keep thinking that," she said. Her grin, if anything, widened.

Vastig had her sword out of line now, thanks to a swift strike at the left side of her face that he'd forced her to parry. He brought his blade's twin toward her kidneys at such speed she would never get her blade back in time to parry—

She didn't. Didn't even try.

Instead, she did the last thing Vastig expected. She kicked him in the gut. A fast, heavy kick, perfect balance and timing. A lesser warrior would have lost his breath to it, especially here in the master's domain.

The kick knocked him three steps backward.

Vastig's arm finished the arc of his swing, but the relic-wielder was out of reach as his sword passed.

It was a good move. A worthy move. Something an elf warmaster would have done. Perhaps an older dwarven sergeant. But a human? Surely not. Surely it was—

"All my life," the relic-wielder said as she closed with a series of rapid attacks that kept Vastig on his back foot. "Same thing. Too short. A woman. Built for a pleasure house, not a battlefield."

Vastig twirled in place, whipping his blades through a series of high and low strikes at such speeds that one of them *had* to land.

Instead she parried the first strike hard enough to throw the second off its line. She then slipped just out of the second blade's path and stabbed inward, breaking the pattern and forcing Vastig back on the defensive.

And all the while she kept talking and grinning.

"I've heard how lucky I am. I've heard a million, million excuses from the losers. The ones I leave alive, anyway. They blame the terrain. They blame their old wounds. They blame the circumstances."

"What will you blame when I'm spilling *your* life's blood?" Vastig asked, finding an opening and slipping onto the offensive once more.

Now it was Vastig pressing her back toward the ghouls. Oh, he could have turned her to a wall instead. But the relic, in her hands, was powerful enough that a little assistance would not go amiss.

Besides, Vastig would still deliver the final blow by his own hand. That was all that mattered.

And yet, she kept grinning. And she parried as though she read Vastig's pattern of attacks even before he decided on it.

Impossible. No human could be that good. The relic must have been even mightier than Vastig thought.

"If *you* kill me," the relic-wielder mocked, "I'll be glad to die. It means I don't deserve to live."

"You don't," Vastig said, hoping to wipe the grin from her face just once before he found the opening that would take her life. "You wield a great relic. Without its powers at your disposal, you would be nothing. You would have died by my arrow on the hill. You would never have sensed me following you. It is the relic and its might that make you a foe worth killing."

She had the temerity to laugh.

"Great relic? It's a fine tool, but it's only a tool. Nothing without the right hand to guide it."

Only a dozen steps to that dome and the ghouls surrounding it. Beating on it. But her words could not go unanswered. Vastig redoubled the force behind his strikes. That would slow his hands a little, but her *arrogance*...

"Never," he said as another notch sheared from his blades when she parried his strike. "It's proven its power to warn you. To—"

"You want to know what powers this sword possesses?"

"Yes!"

Vastig had her now. Her sword out of line. A single thrust would—

The grinning woman shifted her grip. Her sword whirled back on the attack faster than Vastig could follow. As though she needed only think of the movement and the sword would leap to her service. As though the sword were weightless.

Vastig abandoned his strike. Used both blades to parry. But for all the quality of his swords, they'd grown notched and weaker through the fight.

The wyrding black blade cleaved right through them. Sliced Vastig open, from the ribs through the guts and out the other side.

The sword came out of him, and Vastig saw that not a single drop of blood clung to the blade.

The last words he ever heard were, "It can cut through damn near anything."

Cavan still felt stiff and sore from the attack of that thing. That vargamort.

Worse, Cavan felt torn *inside*. As though the necromancer's spell had ripped the core of Cavan's being right down the center.

Worse yet, that spell seemed to cut him off from his own magic, even while it duplicated the necromancer.

Now there were two of the old man, both fighting like young men, swiping and stabbing with their bone wands as though they were blades.

At least Ehren and the others were safe from those ghouls, inside that golden dome Ehren had conjured up. How long it would keep the ghouls at bay, Cavan couldn't be sure, but he had no doubt that even now Amra was devising a plan that would turn the tide.

Amra. For all her taunting and teasing ways, she was the reason Cavan was still alive right now. It was her intensive training — far and beyond the rudiments Cavan had been taught by Ser Dreng, back when Cavan was failing to become a warrior — that kept his hands moving through parries without the need for his mind to get involved.

It was Amra's training that taught Cavan to read the movements and patterns of a foe's strikes. To parry, yes, but also to turn that pattern against the enemy.

Even torn asunder inside, Amra would already be on the counterattack.

Cavan wasn't as good. Especially right now, when he felt so … cloven. Unable to bring himself together enough to mount the kind of counterattack Amra would expect of him.

The most Cavan could do was keep his blades parrying. But that kept him alive. For now, at least.

That spell. It had cut him off from his magic. What else had it done? Was it the *source* of that twinned necromancer? What exactly *was* that spell?

Not something Cavan had time to consider as the necromancer pressed him slowly backward toward the edge of the red, glowing ring of the pentacle graven into the floor beneath him.

Some deeply entrenched instinct told Cavan he must not let himself step on the circle. He didn't know why. Couldn't remember. Couldn't really think properly at all.

But right now, stepping on or through that circle was bad. He knew that much. And in the moment, Cavan could only trust to what he knew that thoroughly.

"An enchanted sword, and a spelled dagger," the necromancers said, in unison. "And the dagger carries your own signature. Not quite a warrior, yet not quite a wizard, are you?"

No time to answer. No time to think. Only time to keep his blades moving. Only time to keep that bone wand from touching him. Even if Cavan gave more ground to do so.

He was getting closer and closer to the outer ring that surrounded the star. He'd leapt over it to enter. He remembered doing it. But that was not an option now. Something had changed.

"You will make a fine protazzon," the necromancers said.

That was a word Cavan recognized. A kind of champion among the undead, wielding both spells and swords against the living.

Was that the answer? The cleaving spell? The necromancer fighting him with both melee and magic together? Yes. Protazzons were a rare form of undead. Likely they had to be made a specific way.

If only Cavan could put the pieces together, maybe the puzzle would make sense.

Closer and closer Cavan came to that edge as the necromancer pushed his attack. And Cavan could hear the ghouls shrieking battle cries. Fighting something now.

A bad sign. Those ghouls weren't likely fighting each other.

The golden dome came down.

His friends were in danger. What could he do?

Nothing. Couldn't think. Could barely fight. It took all his focus to parry those bone wands, fast as they came on the attack. High and low, low and high, middline attacks blended into the mix.

Facing one necromancer was bad enough, but two seemed too much to ask of anyone.

The necromancers spat out a spell then. Another horrific combination of syllables that Cavan's brain refused to take in. But a stream of something white and ghostly issued from the mouths of the necromancers, right at Cavan.

One of those moments in life when time itself seemed to slow.

Cavan couldn't touch his spells, so no way to counter whatever the necromancer was doing. Ducking wasn't an option either. It would throw off his parries, because those wands kept coming.

Cavan wasn't wizard enough to overcome the necromancer's magics, especially right now. Wasn't warrior enough to outfight the necromancer and his spirit image combined.

And now the twin streams of ghostly matter joined together as they came. They tore at the thin air itself as they flowed toward Cavan's face.

Screams came from inside that spell. Screams of the tormented dead, those poor spirits forced to not only serve the necromancer, but to slay at his command. To rip and rend the spirits of those who still had bodies of their own. To prepare the way for the necromancer's fell magics to revive Cavan as one of their own.

Worse. As a protazzon, who would doubtless be turned immediately against his friends.

And even as that spell came at him, the necromancers' bone wands continued their assault.

Nowhere even to retreat now. Cavan's boots were all but touching the glowing blood red ring of the star on the floor behind him.

Cavan saw only one chance.

Cavan doubled the strength of a double-parry. Bought himself fractions of a second.

He dove desperately forward to his right.

The spell soared through the air behind him — close enough to hiss across the back of his neck — and tore into the stone wall, rotting it away as though centuries passed every second.

Cavan tried desperately to think as he rolled, his blades tucked in tight to keep them safe and out of his body. He would need them soon enough. Already the twin necromancers were turning. Approaching. Raising their wands.

Cavan rolled again.

The necromancers fired off another twinned spell that smote the stone floor where Cavan had been moments before. Was his back smoking? The floor was. And something in his back hurt...

No time for that. He had to keep rolling. Had to buy time to puzzle through something that just occurred to him.

He felt a fleeting recollection of Reesa evading Kolsach in her duel. Hoped there would be something like uneven cobblestones to aid him now...

The star on the floor. It was five-pointed like all those used by the Order of the Blessed Star, not seven-pointed like those usually used in necromancy. And yet, the necromancer had chiseled away every star the order had left.

Every star but *this one.*

Why had he left this one star engraved in the floor?

Because he needed it for something.

It was a gamble. Just an instinct, really, but instincts were about all Cavan had left.

He spun and slashed his *licha* sword across the outer ring of the glowing red circle. The circle resisted, but the masterwork edge and enchantments of the sword did their work.

The blade cut. The edge of the circle split asunder.

Fiery power erupted from the cleft. All the power that circled star had channeled and contained, unleashed all at once.

Some of it was simply wasted. Funneled away in a quick flare of orange light so bright Cavan ached to the back of his skull just to see it.

But the rest of that power, that all went into the necromancer in a single flashing instant.

And it *was* just the one necromancer now. Because as that flare of power struck him, the second necromancer shifted into the spirit of a forest elf woman, and faded away.

The necromancer screamed in pain.

A momentary opening. Nothing more. A necromancer that experienced would adjust quickly to the unexpected influx of raw power. Turn it into a weapon. Long before Cavan could close and run him through, much less recall any of the spells that might have done the job.

But training-honed battle reflexes were faster still.

Cavan threw his spelled dagger straight into the throat of the necromancer.

And just as he had practiced a thousand times, he spoke the keywords of the spell he'd carved himself into its blade.

In the moment, Cavan could not recall the meaning of the syllables he spoke. Not even that they had anything to do with a spell. Only that after throwing that dagger, he had to say those words.

But the power of that spell had long since been committed, graven into the symbols on the blade. And triggered by Cavan's voice uttering the right sounds, the spell did its work.

Green fire roared out from that dagger blade. Burned through the throat of the evil spellcaster, as well as a good portion of his head and shoulders.

The necromancer fell to the floor. His charred head bounced twice as it rolled away.

Well and truly dead.

Cavan stabbed the necromancer's body through the heart anyway. Just to be sure.

CAVAN FELT DULL. LISTLESS. DISTANT EVEN FROM HIMSELF. BUT THE necromancer lay dead at his feet, and that was what mattered.

Cavan looked up, but the ghouls that still moved were fleeing down side tunnels. No longer a threat without their master.

The great big junction room seemed smaller now that it was empty of enemies. Had Cavan really pulled off that jumping spell earlier? How had he done that?

Cavan pondered, or tried to, as he glanced around him in the old, stone tunnels under the ruined monastery.

The rest of Cavan's friends still stood. They looked a bit haggard, but no more than he felt himself.

Well, Ehren looked pristine as always, as though his white clothes had never been *near* dirt. And Amra looked as though she'd gotten through this latest fight without even the indignity of a bruise. She was sweating, and still covered in bits of zombie, but that was about it.

Still, Qalas looked worn from his efforts, and Reesa looked just this side of dead on her feet.

Every one of them still lived. Cavan should have felt happy about that, shouldn't he? Elated? Grateful? *Something?*

He felt ... less than himself. And he was sure he should have been able to think of at least *one* spell. Why couldn't he think of any spells? He was sure he'd trained as a wizard, even if he'd been kicked out of that training long before he could have moved on from apprenticeship.

He figured he should remember some of that training, if he took a moment to do it.

Cavan tried to do just that, as he cleaned his blades and sheathed them. Tried to remember a simple spell to produce a spark and light a candle or some kindling.

He could remember sitting in the small, dank room where Master Powys made him practice. Focusing entirely on the wick of that stump of a yellow candle that was older than Cavan was. Although, honestly, Cavan hadn't been all that old at the time.

"You in there?"

Amra's voice. Followed by snapping fingers, and a slap on the face.

Cavan looked at her. Frowned. When did she come stand in front of him?

"I..." How could he describe this? How could he explain it? He felt cut off from part of himself. From a *large* part of himself.

Cavan tried to focus on the green and gold of her eyes. He could hear the others moving about. Doing things that he should probably have been doing too. Gathering remains maybe, or seeing to wounds.

But Cavan shook his head.

"I'm ... not all here..."

"Ehren!" Amra bellowed in full command voice.

Cavan tried to finish his sentence. Tried to find the words that might explain what he was feeling, but they wouldn't come.

Cavan looked back at Amra, but Ehren stood in her place.

Ehren stretched the skin around Cavan's eyes. Peered in with those clear, incisive pale blues of his. Ehren had moved on to checking Cavan's throat and the top of his head by the time Cavan got another word out.

"Torn..."

"Amra," Ehren said, "seat him someplace and watch him while the rest of us gather what we can. We need to get him out of here..."

Ehren was still saying something, but Cavan lost the train of it.

Amra marched Cavan to a spot along the hallway and sat him down. There was a dead forest elf nearby. Cavan blinked at the corpse.

"Yeah," Amra said, "that was the archer. Arrogant ponce. Idiot gave up all his advantage when he tossed his bow. If he'd kept it he might have turned me into a pincushion before I could get close enough to scratch him."

Cavan nodded. The archer he remembered. Hadn't he seen arrows in a vermillion haze? When had that been? How?

"Pretty good with those swords," Amra continued. "Probably a warrior once. But he was too used to fighting like a hunter. Too used to ambushes and quick kills. Forgot about the ebb and flow of a proper swordfight. Fell into old patterns too quickly."

Amra could make anything a lesson. Cavan tried to pay attention, but his focus kept drifting...

"Hey," Amra said, crouching down and lowering her voice against the background clatter and hubbub of activity. "That elf kept calling my sword a 'relic.' Seemed to think it's got powers I don't know about. Think when we have time, you can help me..."

Amra's sentence faded away as she took a closer look at Cavan.

She chuckled. "You're not going to remember any of this, are you?"

"No," Cavan said. "I mean yes. I mean—"

"Forget it," she said, clapping Cavan on the shoulder and standing up. "We'll talk about this later."

"Come on," Qalas said, and Cavan realized the other three were trudging closer now. "We've got the remains of the knights."

"And we need to get ourselves and our horses back to some real air," Ehren said. He brought up the rear now.

The air. Something about the air that Cavan should have known. But for the life of him, he couldn't think of it.

"What about the raiders?" Amra asked.

"They'll have to wait," Ehren said. "We can come back tomorrow, when the sun's up." His eyes flicked to Cavan. "He's in no shape to face ghouls again anyway, and those ghouls are down here somewhere."

The remains. The raiders. Curse it all, why couldn't Cavan think?

Amra whistled for Cavan's attention.

"Let's go, recruit," she barked in her training tones. "Gotta stand before you can walk. Gotta walk before you can run."

Cavan stood without thinking. He even managed to walk a bit. But his focus kept drifting and his feet stopped every time.

Reesa finally had to lead Cavan out of the lair of the necromancer.

10

CAVAN AND HIS FRIENDS CAMPED THAT NIGHT ON A HILL THAT LOOKED so healthy it practically glowed, after all the death he'd seen in the last day or so.

Cavan might not have had the focus to ride well, but he could manage to stay in the saddle, and Dzint was smart enough to do the rest.

Even mounting Dzint had been glorious. A breath of fresh air. They'd ridden for hours before Cavan made the connection that mounting Dzint had provided a *literal* breath of fresh air. The feathers, and their air elementals.

Hadn't Cavan done that? Called the air elementals? Bound them temporarily into the hawk feathers?

Another memory, just out of reach. Like a dream that had faded in the morning light. All he knew of magic, just a faded dream.

Back at camp, Ehren examined Cavan some more, but Cavan didn't even try to pay attention while it happened. Just stared off at the stars and let his thoughts drift wherever they wanted.

Magic. Swordplay. Riding…

Stars. Reesa. Polli…

The necromancer. His archer. The vargamort…

The vargamort. Polli. Reesa...

Somewhere in there, Cavan fell asleep.

His dreams were wild, excitable things that night. Unhinged and inconsistent, but full of meaning and depth and all the answers Cavan could have ever wanted in his life.

If only he could remember anything more about them when he woke.

Cavan roused to the sounds of Ehren's prayers, to realize that he lay in the center of a circle of candles, each a different shade of the sun's coloring as it moved through the sky.

Cavan was naked. Lying on a cloth of gold blanket that he had never seen before in his life.

He could smell ... oil. Sunflower oil. Had someone been...

Symbols, of course. Drawn up and down Cavan's body in sunflower oil.

The taste of orange juice was on his tongue. Couldn't have been from one of the blessed oranges. Ehren always insisted they had to be consumed deliberately to have their proper effect. Still, Ehren must have dribbled orange juice into Cavan's mouth as part of what he was doing.

Now Cavan realized he could smell incense too. Incense? Cavan wasn't sure he could remember the last time Ehren had used incense. He was swinging it in time with his chants, and golden smoke issued forth. Smoke that smelled like a hot summer day.

Smoke that did not rise, but flowed down to circle Cavan, weaving in and out of the candles as it went.

Then, it was as though each candle had its own tendril of smoke, reaching out to Cavan, but stopping short of his body.

He could feel them though. How could he feel them? He felt as though he should have known the answer, but it eluded him.

Anointing oils. Incense. A circle of candles. Cavan had never seen Ehren do anything so involved as this anywhere but a temple. Usually the smiling priest just prayed, perhaps gestured.

Reesa was sitting down by Cavan's feet, looking at him with a worried expression.

Cavan started to sit up without thinking about it.

Qalas and Amra each grabbed a shoulder and thrust him back down.

Huh. Those two were kneeling right up by Cavan's head, just on the other side of the ring of candles. Almost as though they'd expected him to do something like sit up.

"He's been praying since the first lightening of predawn," Amra said softly. "If you move and mess this up..."

Cavan started to raise his hands in surrender, thought better of it, and gave her a deliberate nod instead.

"Good man," she whispered, as the harsh syllables of Ehren's prayers in Penthix grew louder.

"Doesn't matter what he *says*," Qalas said. "Ehren said he'll forget and—"

"I know," Amra said. "But it's easier if he tries to cooperate."

The first rays of dawn crested the horizon. Ehren's prayers sang out loud and clear. Might have echoed for miles, from the sound of them.

Cavan would have sworn those first rays struck only him. Bathed him in their golden radiance, while Ehren continued to pray.

The whole world looked golden to Cavan now. He started to sit up — just a reflex — because the rising sun likely meant the ritual was finished. Ehren's healing always happened in Zatafa's first rays.

But Qalas and Amra shoved Cavan back down, and Ehren kept right on praying.

The sun continued to rise, lighting up the green and golden grasses of the hill around them and lightening the blues of the sky above. Somewhere nearby, a horse whickered. Ondiq. Cavan was pretty sure that was Ondiq's whicker.

And through it all, Ehren's prayers continued. His voice rose and fell. Now chanting, now singing. Always slowly circling, and keeping up that flow of incense.

The rays of the morning sun felt warmer on Cavan's skin than he expected. Closer to the warmth of high summer than fall.

And that warmth, it didn't stop at Cavan's skin. It seeped on down into his muscle and sinew. Into his bones and his blood. The warmth eased inexorably down inside Cavan reaching down to the core of his self, where the worst damage had been done.

When the heat reached that part of him, he cried out in pain. It didn't feel like warmth now. It felt blazing hot. Burning. Singeing. How could this be good? How could anything about this be good?

He tried to get up, but someone was holding his shoulders. And his feet.

He tried to thrash, but his limbs weren't moving right.

And his eyes. He couldn't see anything but gold now. That golden glow was everywhere. It was as though the whole of the universe was golden.

And painful. Searing. Blazing. Burning.

Wait.

The pain was receding now. Ebbing away, slow and smooth as a tide.

The warmth remained though. A different quality of warmth now. It soothed through Cavan. It didn't really feel like *healing* though. It didn't feel the way it did when Zatafa's power helped Cavan's wounds reknit themselves.

It was more...

More of an *invitation*. As though the parts of Cavan's deepest self were being soothed, and gently reminded that other parts existed. Invited to investigate those parts. To rejoin with them.

The sun was fully above the horizon by the time Ehren stopped praying. And by then, Cavan could feel himself coming together once more.

He started to rise.

"No," Ehren said, his voice hoarse from his efforts. "Stay where you are until you feel entirely yourself again. We both..." He yawned. "We both need more rest."

***

It was nearly midday by the time Cavan felt ready to rise and dress. Ehren yet slept, in the shade of a small maple tree near the horses.

Qalas and Amra discussed something in hushed tones, and Reesa stood looking away from Cavan, southwest into the distance, as he rose. She didn't turn around until he spoke.

"Spirit double!" Cavan said, as he fastened his brown riding breeches. "That was the spell the necromancer used against me. A kind of close echo."

Cavan frowned. "Different spin on it though. I swear he used the damage he'd done to me to power it."

All three of the others who were awake looked over at Cavan. All three looked glad to see Cavan up and about, but Amra still managed to be amused by him.

"Figures your first words are about a spell."

"What do you expect?" Cavan said with a smile. "My memories are starting to catch up to my skills."

Amra snorted. Started to turn back to Qalas.

"Hey," Cavan said, slipping into his older, brown tunic. "It was your pushing my martial skills that kept me alive long enough to find an opening."

"I only showed you the way," Amra said. "You had to learn the lesson." She smiled. "But thanks."

The sudden show of grace to a compliment almost threw Cavan off of spitting out the other answers to questions that had occurred to him while he couldn't think straight.

"Protazzons," he said, tucking his tunic into his breeches. "The necromancer wanted to make me one, and he had to kill me through magic and martial means combined. That's why they're so rare."

Cavan yanked on his calf-high, leather boots.

"And the tendrils of smoke from those candles. They were working into the outer edges of my aura. Holding one part of me, while you guys held down my body."

Cavan slipped on his sword belt and fastened it as he continued.

"The star on the floor. Five pointed, because it was part of what few magics the necromancer still mastered that were not tied entirely to death. Movement magic, yes, but more importantly ways of gathering and channeling power *without* relying entirely on death for it."

Cavan shook his head, remembering the feel of that star's glowing magic.

"He must have been planning something big. Felt like multiple wizards had channeled power through that star. Bet it had been used that way by every evil occupant since those monks were killed off or chased away."

"Killed," Reesa said, then shrugged. "That's the one point all the stories agree on."

"Anything else you find yourself suddenly remembering?" Amra asked, and she sounded a little too casual about the question.

Cavan found himself thinking about the vargamort, and Polli, and Reesa. But he didn't think that was what Amra was asking about.

"I don't ... think so. Why?"

"No reason," Amra said with a shrug. "Thought you might have had some great insight about the forest elf or something. You stared at his corpse long enough."

"I did?"

"Well, *near* his corpse. I was never quite sure where your attention was."

"Did you know," Ehren said, still sounding tired, "that the lot of you talk loud enough to *wake* the dead?"

"Well," Amra said, standing. "If we're all awake, let's go see about the rest of those remains."

"You just want to kill off the rest of the ghouls," Qalas said, rising.

"Well," Amra said with a half-smile, "I'm not *opposed* to that. And I do recall *someone* saying we had to deal with that trapped entrance before we leave the area."

Amra fluttered her eyes. "Also. And this is just a thought. Perhaps we ought to at least *try* to finish this quest before the god of death strikes us all down."

That alone was argument enough to get them all on horseback and riding once more.

But before they did, Ehren cleared his throat for attention.

When everyone was looking at him, he spoke with the most somber expression Cavan had seen on the smiling priest for some time.

"Let us be clear about something. The incense I needed for that rite this morning requires sunflowers that only grow in three places on this continent. They must be harvested on the morning of the winter solstice by a priest who intends to spend the next month in isolation, praying and combining them with ingredients I won't even name here and now, in order to *make* that incense. And only the priest who makes it, can use it."

Ehren raised one eyebrow in that way he had. As though he was asking a question without asking it. Rendering judgment without judging. That one eyebrow made Cavan twist with guilt at having made Ehren spend so valuable a resource on him.

"What I am saying," Ehren said, his tone gentler now, "is that am now *out* of that incense. There is no more of it, even in my backpack. And I would very much appreciate it" — Ehren looked straight at Cavan as he said that — "if I do not find myself *needing* more of it anytime soon."

"I'll do my best," Cavan said. Amra and Qalas said something similar, which he appreciated, since he was pretty sure Ehren's warning was mainly for him.

"That's all I can ask," Ehren said, smiling once more as he mounted Highsun. "Now, let us see about ghouls, traps, and a quest from the god of death."

As they rode back toward the ruined monastery, Cavan watched the world once more through his wizard sight. And he was glad to see that the necromantic influence was already beginning to pale.

Oh, on its own it would take months, perhaps years, to fade entirely. But no more active waves of death magic issued forth from the source.

Cavan still intended to inform a temple of the Green Lord of what had happened here. No doubt they would send a priest to speed the recovery.

As things now stood, those flora and fauna that were undead

suffered under the light of day without fresh influxes of necromantic power to reinforce them.

The undead grasses, trees, and bushes would not last long, but the animals could take shelter. Survive longer, if they could find another source of sustenance by preying on living creatures. Likely they would have to spread out from this area to do so.

All the more reason to call for a priest of the Green Lord.

In the meantime, though, the air was breathable again. Cavan had handed his feather to Reesa as they rode, just to test, and sure enough, the air was all fresh and clean once more. Restored by the winds, without more death magic to eat away at it.

Ehren even recovered his voice enough to start singing on the ride, which was a mixed blessing, as ever.

Once they arrived at the ruins, Cavan gathered up the feathers, thanked the elementals, and released them to return whence they came.

The trapped door in the stone floor near the back of the monastery wasn't trapped anymore. Must have had only a magical trap set on it, and that trap did not outlive the necromancer.

Cavan pretended to disable a physical trap all the same, just to avoid getting teased by Amra.

In the catacombs beneath the ruined monastery, only the ghouls remained to pose any kind of threat. The rest of the necromancer's undead had fallen to raw bones the moment he died.

And the ghouls, well, they were disorganized without a leader, and few enough that Cavan and his friends dispatched them easily. Even Reesa held up her end of the skirmishes. She'd come a good way in a short time, so she either had a knack for it or had gotten more tutelage from Amra than Cavan had noticed.

The sun was down, but the moon not yet risen when Cavan and his friends emerged once more from the catacombs into the night air.

Gathered within Ehren's pack they had the remains of all risen dead they could gather from the necromancer's lair. They felt confident that they'd found the bones of all the raiders they'd seen in the ghostly battle, but to be safe they gathered as well the bones of every other fallen former member of the necromancer's retinue.

In fact, the only remains they did not gather were those of the necromancer himself, and the forest elf who served him.

"Seems unfair," Reesa said, as they mounted their horses once more.

"What does?" Cavan asked, expecting something about the poor souls whose remains had been abused for the necromancer's fell purposes.

"We hunted a necromancer down in his lair. Slew him and his right hand man. To hear the bards tell it, there should have been treasure. Piles of gold. Fantastical objects. Wonders."

Cavan laughed. He couldn't help himself. And he wasn't alone. The others all laughed with him, and soon Reesa was laughing herself.

"Never does work out the way it does in the stories of the bards," Cavan said.

"We did find some coins," Qalas said. "Though probably no more than the dead were buried with."

"Besides," Amra said, ever practical, "what would a necromancer want with gold? The guy basically lived in a crypt."

"If you can all it living," Qalas added.

"And the few enchanted things he did have," Cavan said quickly, "were not ones you would want. Believe me."

"Is that why you broke that mirror with that bone cup?" Reesa asked.

Cavan nodded. "And you don't want to know what they were used for."

Reesa swallowed. Nodded.

"Didn't stop you from taking his spellbook," Qalas said.

"I didn't want to leave it there for someone to stumble on," Cavan said. "And that second volume was a journal. Never know what *that* might hold."

"He has that adventure look in his eye again," Qalas said to Reesa.

"Can we find a psychopomp first?" Amra asked. "I can't believe *I'm* the one reminding you that a god will strike us down if we don't."

And then, Cavan and his friends were riding once more, determined to make their camp on fresh, entirely living grass before they slept that night.

11

Cavan and his friends returned to the main road through Holfast — Reesa confirmed Cavan's recollection that this country was Holfast — and continued west, seeking a temple of Istanlos.

They rode past farms and a couple of small towns that were little help except to say that the capital had temples to most of the gods, and that Cavan and his friends should continue westward.

The waning moon seemed narrower each night above their encampments, which did little to encourage Cavan. And it was a statement about their urgency that not one of them — not even Reesa, the least used to sleeping on hard ground — suggested staying in an inn instead of sleeping beside the road.

They all agreed that covering as much ground as they could each day was more important than a little extra comfort.

On the third day along that road, near the point where the river Holrush began to widen, Cavan and his friends finally found Field-send, the capital city of Holfast.

Like the river, the city widened on its way south.

Toward the northern end, past the main road, it began as the fields and farms on either side tapered away. At the southernmost point, where the city was widest, lay the royal castle, where Queen Sarina kept her court.

The castle looked tall and formidable, even from the road, with several towers and visible catapults and scorpions on the stone walls. Walls that extended all the way around the city, and stood tall enough that even an ogre would have to stand on the shoulders of another ogre to reach the parapets.

There were, in fact, more farms to the south. Why was the city called—

"They have a lot of trouble with their neighbors?" Qalas asked, staring at the great iron gate in the wall ahead of them.

"Holfast is matrilineal," Reesa answered. "And—"

Amra snorted. "Let me guess. Their neighbors had to learn the hard way that yes, women *can* lead in wartime."

"Yes, that *is* true," Reesa said, hesitantly, and flushed slightly as she continued. "But the castle and walls were reinforced by Queen Heffria, who rightly guessed that her eldest daughter had no head for strategy. Holfast used to extend about another week's ride to the west. As it stands, only the strength of the castle keeps the western border where it is, about two days from here."

Amra started to say something about that, but Ehren smiled and said, "I believe *someone* mentioned that we have some urgency to what we're doing?"

Amra didn't even look embarrassed. Just whistled the advance, and led them on through the gates — open at midday — and on into Fieldsend itself.

Dirt roads in Fieldsend, and buildings made mostly of wood, standing one, two or three stories tall. Like most cities Cavan had been to, this one smelled of cooked food, sweaty populace, and dung of various types.

No order to the city layout that Cavan could see, but Amra must have spotted something he missed, because she'd never been here so far as he knew, but she seemed to have a purpose to her direction.

Maybe one street later, Cavan realized why. And the answer came in two parts.

Much of the traffic that involved carts, wheelbarrows and trade moved north and south through the town. Likely a farmer's market toward the north end, and the tradesmen clustering as close to the castle as they could in the south.

The east, the direction Cavan and company rode from, held barracks and at least some portion of what looked like a royal army, as well as the city watch.

That made the west the most likely location for any temple not dedicated to Zatafa. Temples to Zatafa, of course, were always as far east in a town or city as they could be, to be closest to the rising sun.

The second part of that realization came from the building designs themselves. The inns and houses, shops and workshops and such mainly had the rectangular designs that humans favored, and the vast majority of this city's populace was human.

But ahead, Cavan could see at least one dome. And he thought he could make out the curving walls that might indicate a temple to Ulsina, the Lady of Ways.

Two blocks later, Cavan was sure of it. That stone structure had the curves and arches of a temple to Ulsina. And that would be the start of the temple district.

From there, Ehren took the lead. The gods had a pecking order of their own, and that manifested in the way temple districts organized, modified sometimes by how revered a god was in a region.

Sare, god of war, always had His temples set as close as possible to the nearest battlefield — west, in this case — with His highest rites performed during the blood red of sunset.

Istanlos was the exception. Cavan could never tell the logic or hierarchical rules that led to the locations of the god of death's temples.

Ehren, however, had no such troubles. He navigated through the busy streets as though he'd been to Fieldsend every summer since he came of age.

The temple of Istanlos in Fieldsend lay at the northwest edge of the city, right in the shadow of the wall. To get there, they had to ride through narrow streets between poorly maintained buildings.

Mismatched wood, patchy roofs. The housing of the poor. Beggars filled those narrow streets, and Amra spat a curse when she saw that some of them were missing limbs. Likely former soldiers, discarded when they could no longer fight, a fact she confirmed quickly enough with gestures from the common battle sign language in this part of the world.

What coins Cavan and his friends had found in the catacombs — and the majority of what other coins they carried — they gave to those in need, with Amra making sure that every old soldier got at least enough for a meal.

At last, though, they arrived at the temple of Istanlos.

———

Most of the temples in Fieldsend were large, grand affairs. Two- to four-story tall stone structures — large enough to host their rituals indoor or out — with ornate sculptures, fine engravings, and the like.

None of this was true of the temple of Istanlos. The god of death tolerated no frivolity. Simplicity was key. Cavan had never been inside a temple of Istanlos, but he understood that much about His worship.

The temple had only the one story, and didn't look big enough to hold more than four rooms total. From the outside, all of the stone used to build it looked rough and irregular, as though taken from cast-off chunks of stone used to build other buildings.

No windows. No glass. And only the one engraving: a single human skull, the symbol of Istanlos, above the open doorway on the left hand side, as they approached.

A temple of Istanlos was always to be entered from the left, and exited to the right. Cavan didn't know why, only that it was so.

No hitching post for horses. Cavan was about to mention that when Reesa spoke, her voice subdued.

"If none of you mind, I would rather not go in. I lost a cousin no more than a season past. We ... we were like sisters. I am not ready—"

"That's fine," Ehren said, managing to sooth without condescension in that way he had. Something about being a priest, Cavan guessed. "You stay with the horses. We'll return soon."

The doorway was narrow, only allowing passage for one at a time. Amra led the way inside, followed by Cavan, Qalas, and then Ehren.

Inside, the room was lit only dimly, by black tallow candles in sconces on the wall. The interior looked as rough and cast off as the exterior. Unmatched benches of hardwood lined the edges of the small room.

Cavan expected the temple to smell like a tomb. Musty, perhaps. But it did not. It smelled like lilies, the flower sacred to the god of death, even though none of them were in evidence.

No one awaited them. No greeter, or acolyte standing ready to minister to those in need.

That seemed odd to Cavan, but before he could say anything he heard a soft gong echo somewhere ahead.

Moments later, he could hear the soft scuffle of shoes on stone.

Finally, a young woman entered the room. No older than Reesa, with the tawny skin of a southerner, though not as dark as Qalas. Her head was shaved bald, and her robes were simple, of undyed rough-spun and bound with a length of cord. Around her neck, only a small skull carved from bone — no larger than the last joint of Cavan's thumb — on a leather thong.

"Welcome," she said. "Are you in need?"

"After a fashion," Amra said, her voice more subdued and respectful than Cavan expected. Sufficiently so that Ehren's eyes rounded wide in surprise. Amra continued, but was quickly interrupted.

"We—"

"You are Amra, Cavan, Ehren, and Qalas. I do not see Reesa."

"She lost someone recently," Ehren said, "and wished to remain outside."

"A moment," the woman said, and stepped past them to the doorway, where she looked outside and nodded. "I had to confirm her participation."

"Of course," Ehren said. "We expected nothing less."

Cavan chose not to point out that he hadn't expected that at all. Though perhaps he would have, had he thought about it. He liked to think so.

"You have brought the remains?" the woman asked.

"We have the remains of those killed in that battle, and more besides," Ehren said, patting his backpack. "Every corpse forced to rise and serve that necromancer."

"The ones we could find in his catacombs, at least," Cavan said. Then, when everyone looked at him, he continued, "It's likely he sent some out on missions that never returned. There's no way to track them all down."

Cavan frowned. "Well, at least there is no way to do it before the dark of the moon."

"Of course," the woman said. "I shall fetch the psychopomp."

"You are not a psychopomp?" Ehren asked, sounding surprised.

"Not until the darkest night of the year will I face my final trial and be confirmed. At this moment, I am only an acolyte."

The acolyte turned and left the room, her sandals scuffling softly on the stone.

"She feels like a priest," Ehren whispered. "This might be a—"

But Ehren's words halted midsentence when they heard the sound of boots approaching. The click of hard heels on stone.

A man strode into the room then. He looked even older than the necromancer, with the many winkles scattered across his pale, pale face. His scalp so bald it almost looked like a skull itself.

But he dressed in the same manner as his acolyte, save for his footwear.

He, too, looked far sprier and more energetic than Cavan expected for a man of his obvious advanced age. Perhaps there was something in the waters around here?

"Be welcome," the psychopomp said in stentorian tones. "Please present the remains."

"They aren't well organized, I fear," Ehren said, taking off his backpack. "I've done what I can, but—"

"Istanlos can pick out every individual in a mass grave, even if it has seen constant use since the days of the Dunaians," the psychopomp said. "Dump them on the floor, if you like. The dead do not stand on ceremony."

"You don't consider that disrespectful?" Qalas asked.

"When done by those who faced down a powerful necromancer to retrieve those remains and bring them here?"

"But—"

The psychopomp scoffed. "The dead care only what happens to their *spirits* once they're gone, not their *bodies*."

"But isn't raising the dead—" Cavan started, but didn't get to finish.

"*Abusing* those remains offends Istanlos," the psychopomp said harshly. But then he smiled. "But whether or not a few bones jumble together does not. And as for the spirits attached to these bones" — the psychopomp shook his head — "it's the abuse *they've* suffered that matters most."

Ehren nodded with a somber expression, and began pouring bones out of his backpack.

It was a sight to see, the way those bones just kept coming out of that leather backpack. Some still attached, like the bones of an arm and hand to a rib cage here. Some all on their own, like the stream of fingerbones that came out at one point.

By the time he was finished, the pile stood half of Cavan's height, and spread out almost the reach of his arms.

All of those bones coming out of that normal-looking backpack. Under another circumstance, it might have been comical.

And yet, the psychopomp said not one word about the backpack.

When the last bone joined the pile — and how Ehren could be so certain that all the bones were out was only one of the mysteries of that backpack — Ehren slung the backpack back onto one shoulder and spoke.

"What else can we—"

"Nothing else is required of you," the psychopomp said. "When I am finished here, I shall journey to the site that began your quest and do what needs to be done there."

The psychopomp tilted his head to one side and added, thoughtfully, "and likely establish a shrine to commemorate the appearance of Zirtax in this world."

"We'd make an offering," Qalas said, "but—"

"But you gave your coins to those unfortunates in the streets. Have no fear. Those people need your coins more than this temple does, and your service is offering enough."

The psychopomp swept his arm wide to the side.

"And now you should go. Food and lodging await you at the Red Briar Inn, courtesy of the temple."

There was a door in the wall that had not been there before. If the entrance had been on the left side of the building, this exit would be in the front.

But then, Cavan supposed, it was still to the right of the entrance. If viewed from that perspective.

"May we at least know your name?" Amra asked.

"All psychopomps surrender our names when we devote ourselves to Istanlos."

The psychopomp gestured again to the door.

Cavan, Amra, Qalas and Ehren each, in turn, thanked the psychopomp — Cavan included Reesa in his thanks, he hoped she wouldn't mind — and trooped out through the door assigned for them.

They found themselves on the opposite side of the building from the door they'd entered through. And behind them, only the rough, mismatched stone of the temple wall.

Cavan stared at the wall a moment, blinking. He shrugged.

"To each god, their miracles," he said, quoting a common phrase for anything that couldn't be explained.

"Come on," Amra said, arching an eyebrow at Cavan. "Reesa's waiting, and you two need to talk."

CAVAN AND REESA DIDN'T HAVE THEIR TALK UNTIL HOURS LATER. WELL after everyone had bathed, and eaten, and had a chance to revel in camaraderie without the pressure of completing a task set by a god.

The jests flew fast, and laughter came easily now.

The Red Briar Inn was one of the finer establishments in Fieldsend. Three stories tall, built from an exotic purple hardwood that lent the fine furnishings a rich backdrop.

They each had their own rooms, with copper tubs right in the room, multiple shuttered windows with panes of fine glass, and the services of the inn washerwoman to tend their clothing overnight.

Best of all — in Cavan's opinion — the rooms had wide, luxurious feather beds. The kind of bed he could stretch out on and sink into blissful slumber.

Or ... entertain, for that matter, in perfect comfort. But he tried not to think too much about that when he bathed.

The five of them dined in a private room, where each of them had their own chairs, ornately carved to match the table. Their meal was roast pheasant with a spicy blend of vegetables and complimented the fresh, tasty bread perfectly.

And the ale was so strong and flavorful even Amra pronounced it worthy.

Finally, though, the meal was finished, and their dessert of apples and pears with honey devoured, along with a rich, dark coffee.

Ehren left the table first, saying something about reading, but Amra and Qalas followed shortly.

And then, Cavan and Reesa were alone in candlelight that should have been romantic.

"It seems wrong," Reesa said. "That we should feast so, and sleep in such comfort, when there are those not so far away who will go cold and hungry. If the psychopomp had offered us the coin—"

"No coins changed hands," Cavan said with a slow shake of his head. "The temple of Istanlos *does* accept donations, but it takes no payment for its services. Those who have been helped by His priests often make their own services available to the temple, as offerings."

Reesa nodded, looking at the flames of the nearest white, beeswax candle.

Cavan wanted to begin, but he wasn't sure how. That encounter with the vargamort, and the tales others had told of what forms the vargamort took for them, they'd troubled Cavan. He'd spent much of the last few days on the road thinking about why that was. Why he had seen Polli, and not Reesa, or anyone else.

Polli was nothing more to Cavan than a pretty barmaid he'd met once. He harbored no secret passion for her. He'd scarcely thought about her since the night they didn't share, and he expected she'd thought of him no more frequently.

The only conclusion Cavan could draw was that Polli represented the fruit not tasted. They'd made an assignation, but not gotten to keep it.

It seemed most likely to Cavan that he had seen Polli, not Reesa, in the illusions of the vargamort because Cavan had not yet found the love of his life. Or at least, he certainly did not know Reesa well enough for her to hold that role.

But what he *could* be sure of was that he needed to know Reesa a lot better than he did before he could consider offering her any kind of commitment. And that would only happen if they traveled together.

An outcome Cavan considered unlikely.

But Reesa stared at the candleflame, and Cavan felt he had to begin the conversation.

"Reesa," he started, but she cut right in.

"I'm not cut out for what you do," she said. "The travel isn't bad, but facing death that way. Laughing about it. I don't know how you stand it. If we hadn't been doing something so very important..."

"It's not for everyone," Cavan said. "But—"

"I don't want to go to Sarkis, either. Besides, father will look for me there, and my presence would cause strife in the family, even if my cousins denied it."

"Besides?" Cavan asked.

She turned to look at him now, her brow troubled but her eyes certain.

"I will stay here," she said. "In Fieldsend. The poor need someone to champion them. I can do that."

"That's certainly a worthy cause," Cavan said honestly.

"Let me be the one to approach the temple of the Green Lord, about the state of that area around the ruin. I'll want their help in feeding the poor, and it may help if I can bring them news of a situation they'll want to fix."

"So—"

"I don't expect you to stay here for me," she said, reaching out and stroking his cheek. "Your path is out there. Perhaps when you are ready to settle down…"

"I'll do so in Juno," Cavan reminded her. "I'm to be count there, remember."

"They have poor in Juno," Reesa said, a touch of mischief in her voice.

"They do," Cavan conceded, "but not on the streets like they do here." And Cavan spent the next while explaining to her how Kent had arranged for housing and care for those in need, and how the mines always provided work of one sort or another.

"Juno sounds like quite a place," Reesa said.

"It's not perfect," Cavan said. "No place is. And even Kent's solutions aren't foolproof." Cavan shrugged. "It helps that the whole county of Juno has fewer people in it than this city."

"But the effort is good," Reesa said.

"So I suppose this is it then," Cavan said.

Reesa blinked at Cavan with eyebrows raised high.

"Oh?" she said, her lips spreading slowly in a smile. "You planned on letting those wonderful feather beds go to waste tonight, did you? Because I thought—"

Cavan leaned in and kissed her.

CAVAN, EHREN, AMRA AND QALAS LEFT THE INN THE NEXT MORNING,

setting out east along the road before they would turn their course north again, toward the home of that dwarven smith.

Dawn was only cresting the horizon as they passed through the iron gates at the east end of town, and Ehren did not even need to ask. They all dismounted while Ehren made his prayers.

Cavan joined Qalas in bowing his head respectfully. It seemed the least he could do, all things considered.

Then, soon enough, they were all mounted again and trotting slowly down the road.

"I note we are four again," Ehren said.

"Please," Amra taunted, "Reesa can do better than this lug."

"She's staying to help the poor, isn't she?" Ehren asked.

Cavan nodded. He expected more jokes or questions, but Amra changed the subject instead.

"Well," she said through a deep breath. "I, for one, am glad to be about our own business once more, instead of doing the bidding of a god. I trust we can avoid making a habit of that."

"We can if you can avoid cutting off the heads of any more ghosts," Qalas said, holding back a chuckle.

"Cut off *your* head if you aren't careful," she said, fluttering her eyelashes, though her tone was playful.

Those two continued their back and forth, while Ehren sidled Highsun closer to Dzint.

"Are you all right?" Ehren asked.

"It's better this way."

"Doesn't make it easy. If you need to talk."

"I'm surprised he *can* talk," Amra chimed in. "After the howling he was doing all night."

"Honestly," Qalas said, "it was like a two-wolf concert."

"No," Amra said, "that's not it. More like a bull moose and a—"

Ehren clapped Cavan on the shoulder as Amra and Qalas found their avenue for teasing after all. For a moment, Cavan thought he had an ally, but then Ehren joined in the fun.

Cavan, chagrined, shook his head. He knew better than to interrupt. They'd grow bored of the game soon enough, if he didn't interrupt.

Besides, that last night with Reesa had been worth all the teasing they could throw.

Now Cavan was on Dzint once more, surrounded by his friends, and riding for a purpose. The teasing was just part of the experience. And honestly, if they stopped altogether, he'd miss it.

Not that he'd ever tell them that.

SIGN UP FOR STEFON'S NEWSLETTER

Stefon loves to keep in touch with his readers, and loves to keep you reading. The best way for him to do both is for you to sign up for his newsletter.

Sign up at http://www.stefonmears.com/join

If you sign up for Stefon's newsletter, you get...

- Monthly updates about his publishing and travel schedules
- His latest news, in brief, and answers to reader questions
- A free short story for signing up
- List-only offers and occasional specials
- Plus a free short story every month!

ABOUT THE AUTHOR

Stefon Mears has dealt with air elementals, but not bound any. Stefon has more than twenty-five books to his credit, and he never stops writing. He earned his M.F.A. in Creative Writing from N.I.L.A., and his B.A. in Religious Studies (double emphasis in Ritual and Mythology) from U.C. Berkeley. He's a lifelong gamer and fantasy fan. Stefon lives in Portland, Oregon, with his wife and three cats.

Look for Stefon online:
www.stefonmears.com
himself@stefonmears.com